Dangerous When Wet

A Pride and Prejudice Variation

Jennifer Joy

Dangerous When Wet: A Pride & Prejudice Variation
A Merry Match for Mr. Darcy, Book 1

Published by Jennifer Joy

Edited by Debbie Brown

Email: contact@jenniferjoywrites.com

Contents

Free Book

Want a free novelette?
Join Jennifer Joy's Newsletter!

Chapter One

1 October 1811

Dear Darcy,
I am an absolute dolt!
It is our first day at Netherfield Park, and already I have failed. My sisters have turned against me, and while Hurst does his best to lend his support, he is no match for Louisa and Caroline when they unite against a mutual enemy—me!

I followed your counsel to the letter, having my man inspect the property along with the bailiff and poring over their report with my secretary. In this, my sisters cannot fault me.

However, I failed to stock the empty icehouse before departing from London, not believing it to be necessary at this time of the year—autumn is upon us, for Heaven's sake! And now, unless you can save us

1

from my folly, we shall melt before you arrive next week!

I know I do not deserve your assistance, but any relief you are able—no, that is not the correct word, for I know no one more capable of doing anything than you... Willing! That is just the word. Now, what was I saying...

Ah, yes, any help you are <u>willing</u> to send would forever put me in your debt, although I am indebted to you for so many things, I wonder how I shall ever repay you or even why you continue to associate with me at all.

Your troublesome, miserable, melting friend,
CB

2 October 1811

My Dear Bingley,

I sent my secretary to Dash's ice chamber, and as I pen this message, a horse and cart is transporting a large block of Norwegian ice to Netherfield Park. You should receive it shortly after receipt of this letter.

Nobody with any sensibility should fault you for not anticipating the need for ice in October. I cannot accept the appellation of hero when you are the one seeing to the comfort of your household.

Every failure presents the opportunity to learn and

improve. Let us have no more talk about debts and regrets; I am happy to be of service to a friend.

However, it would be a great kindness if you would make no mention of this exchange to your sisters. You had sense enough to write for assistance, and for that you ought to receive proper credit.

It is my genuine expectation that you and your household will be well settled and refreshed when Richard and I join you three days hence.

Regards,

FD

Chapter Two

I adjusted the angle of my hat, letting a slip of breeze cool my damp forehead and wishing that acceptable attire was not so stifling. From my fitted leather boots and stockings to my tailored coat and cinched cravat, I had precious little skin that was not roasting under at least one layer of clothing.

Richard doffed his hat and swiped his handkerchief over his face. "Beats traveling in a carriage," he said for the third time in as many hours.

Not having the humor to reply in a pleasant tone, I merely nodded and urged my horse forward. Riding horseback in this blazing sun had been *his* idea.

We rode through a market village, and my resentment toward my vestment increased with each passing of a farmer wearing a loose linen shirt and trousers.

"Makes you feel like a stuffed and trussed pheasant

roasting over the fire, does it not?" Richard nodded and smiled at a father pushing his son's head under the spigot of the water pump by the stables. The man pretended not to be delighted when the boy flicked his wet hair at him. *If only a few drops might have reached me!*

"I see no benefit in dwelling upon it. We must be near Netherfield Park." I sought the shade of a hedgerow, a beautiful specimen of thick shrubbery I admired until it ceded abruptly to an open field along the road. Stubby, brown grass stretched as far as my eyes could see. Not one spot of shade.

I longed to tear off my cravat... and a few more pieces of clothing besides. But gentlemen in my position attracted more than our fair share of interest and speculation, and I would rather boil in my breeches than allow it to be said that Fitzwilliam Darcy's appearance was anything less than exemplary.

Were the landowners in Hertfordshire so indolent that they could not properly mark the boundaries of their property? The field had been cut recently—a month or so ago, judging by the length of the sprouting grass—but it had not yet been replanted. Either the owner was negligent or he possessed an enviable foresight in delaying planting until after this freak heat wave had passed. Many landowners would lose their crops this year. Thank goodness, Pemberley was farther north.

Richard turned to me with a roguish grin that told

me he was about to suggest something wholly improper. "Race you, Darce?"

"Over private property, on a field that is likely rife with holes?"

"As if you know the placement of every hole at Pemberley," he scoffed.

I remained unmoved. "At least Pemberley is my property."

Richard waved his arm about. "Did you not say that the estate Bingley let has been empty these three years? Surely, this is his. No gentleman worth his salt would allow such negligence otherwise."

True. But it was too blasted hot to race. "You will not be so eager to race when your carelessness causes injury to your horse."

"If I am careless, then you are too cautious."

I failed to see the insult in that, though it was clear from his tone that one was implied.

Richard sighed in frustration. "One day, you will regret the risk you did not take."

"I doubt that." My responsibility was to minimize risks, not yield to them.

"At Mother's dinner party, you hardly spoke a word, though there were several handsome young ladies from good families present."

"Am I supposed to regret avoiding insipid conversation and false charm?" I refused to be a casualty in my aunt's attempts to lure a wealthy heiress to wed her second son before he was shipped off to the continent. Her selections had pleasant faces, but their conversation had been woefully bland. A man can only endure so much empty chatter about the weather, the stench of the Thames, and the state of the road.

Richard's complaints continued. "You hardly dance at balls!"

To be fair, that was true. It was an ongoing source of resentment for me. Being constantly on display and pursued by blood-thirsty matrons and interfering biddies with nothing better to do than meddle in my affairs had sapped all the joy out of an activity I had once relished. I could not dance without the gossips implying a budding romance with my partner... as if dancing was a certain step towards falling in love.

"And now you refuse to race! You are no fun anymore, Darcy."

That struck its mark, and my bluster deflated in one lengthy exhale. There had been a time when my cousins and I were masters of mayhem. That was before my mother fell ill and it had seemed wrong to laugh at anything. Before I reached my majority and came under harsher scrutiny. Before my father's death, when I was made to understand that my duty transcended my mourning.

The master of extensive properties and a large fortune with relations among the peerage must not let his guard down or disappoint his dependents. For their sake as much as mine, I could not afford to take risks.

"If I am disinclined to indulge in diversions, then you, of all people, must know my reasons."

"Save your withering glare. I know you too well to be cowed by it." Richard's reprimand was softer than his previous accusations. He pretended to grumble, but he ceased his attempts to spur me into racing him.

A copse of trees bunched along a stream provided a more favorable target for our evaporating energies. Directing my horse to the shade of a sprawling oak with roots plunging into the water, I dismounted and let the gelding drink.

Dipping my handkerchief into the water, I splashed my face and gloried in the cool liquid trickling down my neck and soaking into my wretched neck cloth. It was a lovely spot, complete with a rope dangling from a thick branch over the deepest part of the stream. Fifteen years ago, I would have been tempted to swing from it. The memory stirred in my breast.

Richard stood beside me. "I hate it when you do that."

I squeezed my eyes shut and pinched the bridge of my nose. Would there be no end to his grievances? "I heard your complaints. I can neither refute them nor alter my conduct to suit everyone's expectations. Would you have me take risks and encourage hope when there is none?"

"You miss my point completely. When was the last time you laughed so hard, your ribs hurt?"

I remembered, and the memory burned my eyes and swelled in my throat. "Sounds painful," I croaked.

He bunched his cheeks together. "You are intelligent enough to know what I mean."

A duck glided out from behind some reeds nearby, quacking and wiggling its tail. A happy distraction. A Godsend!

I patted my pockets, knowing that the gesture would not produce a pocketful of crumbs but wishing it all the same. My groom only carried apples—nothing befitting a duck. "Do you have any bread with you?"

"I regret that I do not." Richard knelt on the bank, dipping his hands in the crystalline water and rubbing it over his face while the duck swam back and forth in front of us, opening its wings and preening. "I think she believes herself to be the keeper of these waters. Such quacking and flailing. When we mount our horses and depart, she will no doubt congratulate herself on a job well done."

I glanced at Richard from the corner of my eye, certain he was joking. "Would you allow yourself to be chased off by a duck?" I chuckled, though the feigned amusement was more to prove to myself than to him that I knew how. Encouraged by the sound, I added, "My cousin, commander of hundreds, expert fighter, and overall impressive figure"—I paused while Richard's chest swelled—"is terrified of a duck."

Richard guffawed. "A dastardly duck! Do you not see how she trains her beady eyes on me? Napoleon's army could not stir more fear in my breast than that floating fiend. You ought to fear the formidable fowl, too. I tell you, she will not cower before your intimidating presence, no matter how intensely you glower at her."

"My glares are lost on this valiant duck, brave guardian of this charming swimming hole. No, my scowls are better saved for simpering ladies and their conspiring mothers intent on entrapping me into an unwanted union."

"Yes, it must be insufferable to have so many perfectly lovely ladies from which to select." His sarcasm was strong.

"You have the freedom to marry whomever you choose."

"So long as she has a fortune! You are too picky, Darcy, and *that* is your problem."

"According to you, I am replete with problems." This, from a man no closer to the wedded state than me. He was one to talk. "Is that why you are two years my senior and still unmarried?"

He grumbled, as I knew he would, but the reprieve from his haranguing was gratifying.

Feeling quite cool and amiable, I mounted my horse, and we rode a short distance downstream, where the water's depth suited our crossing.

"We ought to return for a swim. I am of a mind to test my skills on that rope swing." Richard eyed me askance, testing my reaction.

"I shall return with some bread for the Queen of the Stream, but I have no desire to swim. We do not know for a certainty if Bingley's property includes the river or not."

"What do you know about Bingley's neighbors? I do not suppose he is so fortunate to have let an estate abutting another property managed by a landed family with a bevy of unmarried daughters?" Richard wiggled his eyebrows.

"If that is the case, I am inclined to conclude from the neglected fields that their father is an indolent gentleman who cares for his property as well as he provides for his daughters. We would do well to keep our distance."

Richard rubbed his chin. "I had not considered that. If that is the case, I declare that the field we crossed must belong to an elderly gentleman with no heir to inherit. Or even more likely—and as I have said from the beginning—it is within Netherfield's boundaries, and we are free to swim there whenever we choose. I rather fancy a swim."

With Miss Bingley nearby? She considered that my friendship with her brother was a certain step toward an offer of marriage, and I could not risk stripping down to my drawers to swim where she might conspire to chance upon me.

"I hear that Miss Bingley is handsome in appearance and in dowry..." Richard began, making me wonder if I had spoken my thoughts aloud.

"You are welcome to her if you can stand her." Richard drove me mad most of the time, but I did not wish him afflicted with a disparaging critic for a wife.

"Unlike you, I do not need to marry a diamond of the first water from the finest family in England. I might just have a go at Miss Bingley."

I shivered. "Pray have more respect for your future happiness."

"Then let us hope that Bingley's neighbors are more promising."

We rode by a pond, which was low and murky from lack of rain. Beyond the pond was a Palladian mansion built of honey-colored Bath stone—Netherfield's grand house.

Having crossed through the field, we took the path which led to the back, and I was pleased to see the tidiness of the lane and gardens surrounding the house.

The windows of the upper floors were tall and wide. Alas, there were no trees to provide shade for the dwelling.

"A proper sudatorium in this heat. Do you think we shall find the Bingleys and Hursts in the icehouse?" teased Richard.

No wonder Bingley had written for help.

Chapter Three

Richard and I followed Bingley's butler into the parlor facing the West end of the house, a generously proportioned room fashionably decorated in a Chinese theme with bamboo tables and figurines painted black and gold.

Richard leaned closer to whisper. "Someone has been to Brighton Pavilion."

Exactly. He must be aware that a lady who imitated the Prince Regent's taste in decor would simply not suit him.

Bingley jumped up from his chair to greet us, cheeks flushed, face beaded with sweat. He appeared to be melting, just as he had stated in his letter.

"You two look as cool as cucumbers! How do you manage it?" He shook our hands and gestured to the armchairs positioned near the open windows.

Miss Bingley rose, a coy smile gracing her lips.

"Ladies and gentlemen of quality never lose their equanimity." She extended her hand to me, pretending an intimacy I had given her no leave to assume.

I took her hand as briefly as propriety dictated without giving offense, but I did not bow over it.

At her sister's declaration, Mrs. Hurst calmed her ferocious fanning and granted us a deferential nod. She flared her nostrils when her husband leaned close enough to benefit from her fanning.

"Shall I ring for some tea?" Miss Bingley again motioned to the empty chairs and established herself as the hostess.

It was too hot for tea, so we politely refused. As unaffected as Miss Bingley attempted to be by the excessive temperature in the parlor, she must have been relieved not to have to serve a steaming beverage.

Richard nudged me as we took our seats, and I took my cue. "It has been many years since you last saw my cousin."

Miss Bingley arched her brow and tilted her chin just so. "Cousin?" Her eyes brightened. "I could never forget a relative of yours, Mr. Darcy."

Ah, so she had made the connection to my uncle, the Earl of Matlock. Richard was not in uniform and I did not recall Bingley uttering his name, but she was not one to forget a peer.

Bingley rested his ankle over his knee, his chair squeaking as he sat back. "How is the viscount, Colonel?"

It was amazing how quickly Miss Bingley's brightness dimmed.

Richard grinned. "He is engaged. Did you not hear? To a lovely young lady from Sussex."

Bingley was delighted at this bit of news, as he was at most things. He loved weddings. Had my aunt been present to discuss the details of the affair, she would have found an attentive audience in my dear friend.

It became clear that Bingley had reached the limit of Richard's knowledge of the viscount's upcoming nuptials. "We should all be so fortunate. Now, how long shall we have the pleasure of your company, Colonel?"

"A sennight, if it is not any trouble."

"Only a week? Have you no more leave?"

"You would persuade me easily enough, but my time is not mine to command."

That honor went to His Grace, Prince Frederick, the Duke of York. My uncle had used his friendship and connections to keep his son doing administrative work at the Horse Guards by securing him a position as an assistant to the recently re-appointed Commander-in-Chief.

Bingley nodded. "You are always welcome in my house. However, since you cannot stay longer, perhaps you will help me convince Darcy to delay his return to Pemberley by another month."

I shook my head firmly. "My sister is expecting me the first week of November."

Bingley sighed. "I cannot ask you to disappoint your sister, though she is more than welcome to join you here."

"Oh, I just adore Miss Darcy!" Miss Bingley gushed. "You must insist that she join us. What a wonderful time we would have! She is such a dear girl."

I could not imagine a worse torture for my shy sister, who had only recently suffered a terrible betrayal. She required the quiet and stability of Pemberley to restore her spirits. I could not stay away from her longer than the month she had insisted I take after concluding my business in London. "Pray give me leave to send your regards in my next letter."

Before she could continue, I turned to Bingley. "I hope you are finding Netherfield Park to your liking?"

Bingley grinned. "It is perfect!"

Of course it was. Bingley loved everything. Of all my acquaintances, he was the easiest to please.

Richard reached over to clap him on the back. "I should say so, and I shall praise your good sense in letting such a fine estate if you can confirm that the charming chalk stream we stopped at on our way here is within your property's boundaries.

Miss Bingley sneered. "Charming, you say? This is hardly Grosvenor Square. I have yet to see anything charming in Hertfordshire."

Clasping his heart as though she had delivered him a mortal blow, Richard teased, "That was a clever cut, madam. Darcy and I both found it a delightful spot. Though my cousin's composure is more expertly trained, I am not as inclined to forgive an offense to my vanity as he is."

The shock on Miss Bingley's face when she realized she had unintentionally insulted us had me biting my cheeks and holding my breath. It also filled me with relief. Richard would not pursue her.

Bingley chuckled. Then, like a good brother, he changed the topic. "You know, I believe the river marks Netherfield's southernmost limit. If I recall correctly from the bailiff's map, the chalk stream you speak of divides my property from my neighbor's. Longfellow, Longshore, Long-something-or-other."

A neighbor who did not fence his field or call on a gentleman recently arrived to settle in the estate bordering his own? What kind of landowner was he? I had to give allowances for the dreadful weather delaying his call, but the gentleman's faults were adding up.

Richard slapped his thigh and stood. "Excellent! We must go explore—perhaps cool ourselves. Unless you have plans to reconvene inside the icehouse?"

I shot Richard a warning glance, but the damage had been done.

"I know you told me not to thank you, Darcy, but" —I cast Bingley a stern look, which he immediately understood—"b-but, I cannot thank you enough for..." He searched around for an appropriate excuse.

"For saving us from boredom? Your timing is impeccable, as always, Mr. Darcy. We would have perished of ennui had you not arrived today."

Bingley latched onto his sister's remark readily, and Richard's smirk grew.

No good deed goes unpunished—a lesson I ought to have learned by now.

It was impossible to be cross with Bingley when his every word brimmed with sincerity. But Richard? He was a fair mark. Given the toothy smile he wore as Miss Bingley added her fawning compliments to her brother's, I vowed to make him pay.

But first, I must quit the room. "What do you say, Bingley? Do you care to join us for a ride to the stream?"

Miss Bingley immediately objected. "But you only just arrived. You will want to settle in your suites and refresh yourselves before we dine. I believe that pork cutlets and apple and barberry pie are your favorites?"

She knew my favorites? As a hostess, she performed her duties admirably, but I was beginning to feel the pinch of expectations.

"Nonsense," Richard said. "Beetroot and Spanish onions with a hearty ragout has always been his favorite."

I tried not to gag. Then, as it became clear that Miss Bingley would put those detestable dishes on the next menu, I laced my fingers to keep from strangling my cousin.

The miscreant locked eyes with me and smiled mischievously, adding, "Besides, it is cooler out of doors than it is in this parlor."

I returned his grin. *And there are fewer witnesses to hear you scream.*

Richard read my look expertly. Unfortunately for me, while I excelled in subtle, silent threats, he had a talent for voicing his publicly. "In fact," he said, his gaze never wavering from mine, "Mr. Hurst and the ladies might decide to join us. We could make it a proper party."

Not since Aunt's dinner party had I been more tempted to launch myself at him. Speaking through my clenched jaw, I responded, "It is cooler, but the sun is intense."

Richard scoffed. "The ladies are not bats or vampires!"

I was too vexed to appreciate the humor in his retort.

Mrs. Hurst continued to stir a feeble breeze with her fan. "I have no desire for unseemly freckles or sunstroke. You gentlemen can go on without me."

That settled, the ladies and Hurst retired while the rest of us changed our coats and agreed to adjourn to the entrance hall in a quarter of an hour.

It was not much time, but it was sufficient. Looking up and down the hall, I made my way to the kitchen. A blast of heat gave me pause and slowed my step.

"Mr. Darcy!" Cook exclaimed, wiping her hands

on her apron to pinch my cheek as she had done since I was a lad.

"Mrs. Ramsay, I pray you are well? How do you find Netherfield's kitchens?"

She patted my cheek and looked about her domain —the polished copper pans hanging from hooks on the wall, the clean tables, and the covered bowls lined near the stove—with button-popping pride. "'Twas in a state at first, but Mr. Bingley gave me carte blanche to whip things into shape. He's a good man, he is. So easy to please."

"Take care you do not overwork yourself in this heat. And, pray, make good use of the ice. The weather will soon turn, and the winter will provide ice enough to restock the stores."

She nodded at the open window and the pitchers sitting on the sill. "I've been putting ice shavings in the raspberry vinegar. The servants know to come here when they feel the need. I daresay we're faring better than Mr. Bingley's sisters."

Remembering my purpose, I extracted a letter from my pocket and handed it to her. "Mrs. Cradock sent this for you."

Mrs. Ramsay fluttered her hands. "Ooh! It must be the recipes I requested! I hope you don't mind your London cook sharing her secrets with me, but I knew you were coming. I wanted to make sure your favorite dishes were up to snuff. I see that her devotion to you exceeds her attachment to her recipes!"

"You and Mrs. Cradock seem to have the sole mission of fattening me up. I shall have to spend all my day in exercise to prepare for dinner."

"Well, we are cousins, you remember! 'Tis our job to keep our masters plump and happy! Happy masters are the best masters. Ah, but you're a good man, Mr. Darcy! The young lady who finally captures your heart is to be envied."

Did nobody think of anything but marriage?

The letter delivered, I secured an end of bread for my pocket and Mrs. Ramsay's assurance that nary a beet would grace my dinner plate. She departed for a shady spot out of doors before the hot work of dinner preparation began, and I rushed upstairs to splash water on my face. Weller, my loyal valet, had my riding kit brushed and polished.

When I returned to the hall, Miss Bingley stood in the center, dressed in a floor-grazing riding habit. A ridiculously long ostrich feather dyed the same color green as her Hussar-style jacket protruded from the side of her black beaver hat.

Motioning at her gold-braided epaulets, Richard looked about the room with one hand at his side, as though he were reaching for his pistol. "Where are the French?"

Miss Bingley pretended to wipe a piece of lint off her shoulder, communicating in one gesture her opinion of Richard. "It is the latest fashion."

"Oh, I do not doubt it, Miss Bingley. However, it

does not suit this weather. I must beg you to reconsider joining us on this excursion."

She opened her parasol, holding it over her head. "I daresay I shall fare better than you, Colonel."

"What of your duties? Is it not the responsibility of the lady of the house to meet with the housekeeper after breakfast?"

"You know a good deal about the subject. Are the duties of a colonel similar to those of the mistress of a house?"

The roguish glint in Richard's eye turned downright devilish.

Without breaking eye contact or understanding the danger she courted, Miss Bingley continued, "I already saw to my responsibilities earlier in the day and am at my leisure."

"Impressive efficiency. You would make a fine soldier."

With a huff, she turned to her brother. "Do you mean to stand here all day, or shall we ride?" She strode out to the drive where a groom scrambled forward with her horse.

Richard nudged me in the arm with his elbow. "If that is what the finest finishing school does to young ladies, you did well to let Georgiana stay at Pemberley. She will fare better in the country than in town with all the parvenus giving themselves airs." He frowned. "Our Georgie needs a wholesome influence—someone bold in the right way."

I couldn't help it. "Like your duck?"

He rubbed his chin. "She is bold, I give her that. Come, let us pray we shall meet Bingley's neighbor and his troop of unmarried daughters."

Richard could dream all he wanted, but the likelihood of finding the one lady capable of engaging in intelligent conversation and infusing me with cheer was nil. At least I would have the pleasure of feeding the duck.

Chapter Four

Bingley was still trying to convince his sister to remain behind when I mounted one of his horses.

Miss Bingley smoothed her hands over her coat skirt and picked at a ruffle on her cravat. "An exceptional hostess should acquaint herself with the property over which she presides, and I"—her eyes flickered to me—"am an exceptional hostess."

She could not have made her meaning clearer, and it was then that I decided I would leave with Richard when he returned to London at the end of the week.

"It is as hot as an oven out there!" Bingley gestured wildly at nothing in particular.

"And yet, you are venturing out."

"You despise being out of doors!"

"I adore nature, and there are few things I enjoy more than riding."

The outright bewilderment on Bingley's face belied the truth of her claim. If she was trying to impress me, she could have saved her breath.

He blustered. "B-But we were going to swim!"

Miss Bingley dismissed her brother's expostulations with a wave of her gloved hand. "Nonsense. Mr. Darcy would never swim in public."

I most absolutely would if for no other reason than to prove her wrong... just not in her presence.

"On my private property!" her brother corrected.

"Come, Charles, we are not rustics who swim in filthy rivers." She urged her horse forward, determined to spoil our plan.

Richard waited until the pair were a sufficient distance ahead of us to speak. "That lady clearly holds certain vain hopes, but I doubt you have given her reason to expect that you notice her any more than a chambermaid."

"I should hope not."

"'Tis a terrible pity. Miss Bingley is handsome and comes with a tempting dowry."

Was he trying to convince himself to pursue her? Richard's repetitions of her only merits irritated me to the point of bluntness. "Bribe money for the poor unfortunate chap desperate enough to marry her."

"Some men tire of fighting, Darcy."

"Then manage my estate in Somerset. You would be doing me a favor."

"I am too proud to live off your charity."

"Foolish pride. The house shall fall into disrepair unless you take it." Any house left unoccupied fell slowly into decrepitude. Everyone knew that. I kept my gaze fixed firmly ahead.

Richard looked at me askance. "A property under your care falling into disrepair? I doubt that."

My jaw tensed. Was Richard serious? I could not in good conscience allow my best friend to surrender to a miserable fate without a fight. How had I failed to notice his discontent?

Twisting in his saddle, Richard laughed. "You are genuinely worried!"

This was not a joke. "Of course I am! You would make each other terribly unhappy, and I wish better for you. Even Miss Bingley deserves to be well-settled... just not with you. Or me."

"Do not trouble yourself on the matter any further. She is too enamored with you to notice me. Nevertheless, I am relieved at your assertion that she has not turned your head. Mother was worried. After all, Miss Bingley is rather fetching." Again, that side eye.

"I prefer dark hair and deep conversation," I grumbled.

"A rare combination."

"I do not intend to marry an ordinary woman."

"No, by your description, you intend to marry someone just like you. Only, I pray you do not. You need someone lively, someone to add noise to your life and color to your obdurate world. Someone fun."

We were back on that topic, were we? Not fun. "Someone unlike you, then?"

"If ever a lady shakes you to your boots, she is the one I declare you should marry."

"You make her sound like a fearsome creature."

"What is an intelligent woman, if not fearsome?"

I conceded the point, but I did not know any such woman. Why should I heed my unattached cousin's advice on a subject he knew nothing about?

Miss Bingley pointed her parasol at a copse of trees at the bottom of a slope in the distance. "Is that the quaint little spot you wished to show us, Colonel? Shall we see if it is as charming as you claim?"

Richard and I took the lead to show the way while Miss Bingley declared every tree, bird, and strand of grass inferior to Pemberley. She had visited my estate only once. I found the accuracy of her memory both impressive and disturbing.

As we rode closer, an unexpected noise made me rein in my horse to hear better. A bird chirp? No, voices. "I think someone might be there." The rest of our party stopped to listen, and I could clearly hear squeals and laughter.

Miss Bingley huffed. "Farmer's children. Come, Charles, do something."

His eyes widened. "Do? What do you expect me to do? If it is children, they are welcome to swim in the river. It is sweltering."

"This is private property! You must defend what is yours."

"It might be ladies," suggested Richard hopefully.

If Miss Bingley disapproved of children playing, she doubly disapproved of the idea that ladies could be swimming in her brother's stream. "A lady would never be so indecent!" she proclaimed, raising her nose in self-righteous superiority. "No lady of quality would make such a ruckus swimming in a murky stream."

For one not born into the gentle class, she believed she knew a great deal about ladylike deportment. Out of respect for Bingley and regard for our friendship, I bit my tongue and, with a look, warned Richard to do the same.

Tapping my horse's sides, I led the way down a well-worn path, twisting through the grove at an easy trot. The joyous cries growing louder as I neared the clearing were a welcome contrast to Miss Bingley's lofty pretensions.

The dirt along the riverbank was dry and soft. Before my eyes had adjusted to the shady copse, the clearing opened wide.

A young lady dressed in head-to-toe blue flannel jumped from her perch atop the tallest root of the oak tree, wrapping her thighs around the rope she held. Out she swung, over the river and up, closer to my side of the bank.

To say she had finely shaped calves would be too restrained a description. One look was enough to determine that she must be fond of activity. Given the disparity between the tan of her face and hands with the pallor of her muscled legs, that activity was most often performed out of doors.

I was about to turn away when she leaned backwards and let go of the rope. My heart stopped, my breath suspended, and I had not the wherewithal to do more than stare at her with open-mouthed shock.

Spreading her arms out like wings, her body flipped around with all the grace of a kingfisher. And still, I gawked. Hardly a dignified aspect, but I had never seen the like of her or the feat she performed. Rolling in the air, she tucked her knees into her chest and landed with a resounding splash directly in front of me, dousing me splendidly.

Water dripped down my face, some of it trickling past my cravat in glorious tendrils of exquisite relief.

My horse, having more sense than myself, had known to stop without my direction. He lowered his head to drink from the stream, granting me an uninterrupted view of the stream and its occupants—all five of whom stared at me in obvious surprise.

I did not know Richard was beside me until I heard his low voice. "A bevy of females. Marvelous!" He removed his hat and swooped it in a mock salute, which the four females bobbing in the river could easily take as a gallant greeting.

An older gentleman sat in the shade of the oak tree, his feet in the water. "Good day to you, sirs," he greeted. He did not trouble himself to remove his pipe from his mouth but instead spoke around it.

My attention remained on the river. The young lady had yet to surface, and I could not rightly spare him or the other ladies a glance until she did. Why had she not reappeared? Did she know how to swim? Most ladies did not, and the water in the center of the river had been too deep to cross on horseback. If she was unable to gain the riverbed and walk ashore, every moment was too precious to waste.

Why did nobody do anything?

Flinging my leg over the saddle, I slipped my feet from the stirrups, my gaze fixed on the spot I thought she might be. Before my boots hit the dirt, she jumped out of the water, pushing herself up and onto the very root where the gentleman sat. Her strength impressed me, but truth be told, the way her bathing gown clung to her curves—turning what would otherwise be a modest, unbecoming, sack-like garment into a form-hugging sheath—captivated me.

Thus, I was ill-prepared for my feet to meet the ground. I had to grasp onto the saddle to catch myself before I lost my balance.

I did my best not to stare at the young lady, but the memory of her twisting through the air before plunging into the stream to emerge with all the elegance of a practiced performer burned my face, singed my conscience, and branded her image on my memory.

Were I to live a hundred years, I would never forget her.

A round of girlish giggles recalled me to my senses, but I had been caught ogling the young lady now sitting with her feet tucked under her beside the man with the pipe. His sardonically arched brow made my stomach twist. He must be her father. And I was making a cake of myself.

I pulled my gaze away, trying to calm the mortification burning in my face and flaming down my neck.

A third young lady wading beside the two giggling ones attempted to quiet them. The fourth squinted her eyes in my direction, her lips pursed in pointed censure.

Bingley positively beamed, and his ability to reply intelligently filled me with jealousy—a sensation to which I was unaccustomed. "It is a beautiful day, is it not?" Along with Richard, he dismounted gracefully.

Miss Bingley pinched her lips and refused her brother's assistance to hand her down.

The gentleman spoke. "Thomas Bennet of Longbourn at your service. These are my daughters: Jane, Elizabeth, Mary, and the two giggling are my youngest, Kitty and Lydia. I regret we are not more presentable, but we had not known to expect company at the stream today."

Bingley introduced himself, after which further introductions could be more properly made. "It is a pleasure to meet you, Mr. Bennet, and your lovely daughters," he concluded, his entire countenance glowing with sincerity.

I bowed, looking anywhere but at Mr. Bennet or Miss Elizabeth. When the task proved too difficult, I occupied myself with soaking my handkerchief.

"My wife will be sorely vexed she was not here to meet you," said Mr. Bennet. "I have been meaning to call at Netherfield Park to welcome you to our humble piece of the shire." He chuckled. "Alas, I reach the stream, and the refreshing water persuades me to go no farther in this dreadful heat."

The gentleman was just as I suspected. He was not the sort to move himself to action unless most of the work was done for him.

Bingley displayed his good nature with his amiable reply. "Then I hope you will call at Netherfield with Mrs. Bennet. You are welcome any time."

"As you are also welcome at Longbourn." Mr. Bennet's eldest daughter said something to him, but she spoke too quietly for me to hear. "Ah, yes, of course you are right, Jane, and I have no doubt that Mr. Bingley will appreciate your thoughtfulness. Netherfield has been empty long enough for its ice stores to melt. I would be happy to share some of our supply."

Miss Bingley chose that moment to speak from the height of her horse's back. "A kind offer, I am sure, but our dear brother thoughtfully had ice brought in from London. When we host our dinners, we shall have ices."

Mr. Bennet's smile remained constant, but I noticed a new puckish gleam in his eye. "How fortunate for your guests. No doubt, your ice is not the impure stuff from ponds and lakes."

Miss Bingley stepped right into his baited trap. She made a derisive snort. "Of course not. Only Norwegian ice is suitable to serve our guests."

Mr. Bennet's eyes shone brighter with every affirmation of her arrogance, as did his daughter's. They were not intimidated by her airs.

"We settle for nothing less than the best," Miss Bingley said, effectively making herself the butt of a joke to which she was not privy. In the eyes of her audience, she was ridiculous. The longer she continued in this vein, the more humorous the Bennets would find her. Hardly the reaction she sought.

Bingley, unaccustomed to receiving his sister's acclaim, laughed awkwardly. "I cannot take the credit when it was Darcy who made all the arrangements. His name has much more sway than mine."

All eyes converged on me. *So much for Bingley keeping a confidence!*

Miss Bingley was not one to allow her compliment to be minimized. "You prove my point, Brother. Only the best, and nobody could claim a better friend than Mr. Darcy."

I shook my head, wishing to disappear.

"Is it your custom to barge in on ladies swimming, Mr. Darcy?" Miss Elizabeth tinged her chastisement with merriment, confounding me further. Was she laughing at me?

Yes, I had assumed she did not know how to swim despite the evidence to the contrary. I had been wrong to assume she was like most ladies. Clearing my throat, I found my tongue. "I beg your pardon, madam. I am not acquainted with many ladies who know how to swim, and certainly none who would flip backwards off a rope."

"Oh, Lizzy does that all the time!" said one of the giggling girls.

"She was not in any danger," added another.

I nodded in acknowledgment of what should have been obvious to me had I been in possession of sense. "It was presumptuous of me to intrude where I was not needed. Pray accept my apology, Miss Elizabeth." My voice cracked as I uttered her name, completing my humiliation.

"I can hardly take offense at a reaction which would be both heroic and gentlemanly under different circumstances, Mr. Darcy. Allow me to assure you that I am an exceptional swimmer. At no time did I require your assistance."

Capable, independent, not in the least awed by my presence. Never had I met her like. "I do not doubt your ability."

"And I have no reason to doubt your sincerity."

I prayed that the redness in my face would be attributed to too much time in the sun. While I would not have hesitated to dive into the river to her rescue, I could not look at her without recalling the curve of her hips and the whiteness of her exposed calf.

Fortunately, she had directed her attention to Bingley by the time the valiant Keeper of the Stream swam out from behind the reeds toward me.

Chapter Five

I pulled the dried bread from my pocket, tore off a piece, and tossed it into the stream. The duck swam closer, wiggling her tail and quacking contentedly between pecks and dives into the water. And Richard and I had made her out to be a fierce protector! She was as docile as the ducks at Pemberley's ponds.

Mr. Bennet said, "This is the best spot to swim in the whole river. As we share it with Netherfield Park, you are welcome to it when we are not here. If you do not mind going a way upstream and do not object to sharing with a family of otters, you would have privacy enough to make yourselves comfortable."

Bingley was charmed at the mention of the otters.

"I am quite comfortable, thank you." Miss Bingley was determined not to find anything agreeable. Her appearance clearly belied her assertion. The ringlets framing her face hung limply against her shiny, ruddy cheeks.

Mr. Bennet arched his brow. "Yes, you appear comfortable." This was a gentleman of astute observation and a mind bent on humor, but—just as the rest of my party at the moment—he did not seem given to action.

Wishing Bingley would quit staring at the fair-haired one long enough to attend to his own sister, I dipped my handkerchief once again into the stream and shoved the dripping linen at Miss Bingley. She was certain to read too much into my gesture, but she could suffer from sun stoke. The guilt and misery she would inflict on her brother surpassed the discomfort her unwanted attentions would impose upon me.

I felt someone watching and looked over to see that it was Miss Elizabeth. With a familiar quirk in her brow, she observed, "It is a fine day for a swim." Her smile eased my embarrassment.

Much to my consternation, the corners of my lips tugged upward. I had learned to be sparing with my smiles over the years, and it disturbed me how easily I returned hers. Again, I had to make myself look away.

"And all of you are accomplished swimmers!" Bingley gushed.

His sister regarded him with disdain. "Knowing how to swim is hardly an accomplishment for a lady."

"On a day such as today, I would argue that it is." Bingley looked at Richard, who nodded his agreement.

Mr. Bennet removed his spectacles and pulled a cloth out of his pocket to clean them. "All my daughters know how to swim, although they do not enjoy the activity equally." He looked at the squinty eyed one.

One of the giggly ones jabbed her in the arm, "He speaks of you, Mary." For our benefit, she added, "Mary would much rather read books of sermons than do anything diverting."

"Of what use is a strong body if the mind is weak?" Miss Mary contested.

"Equally frustrating is a strong mind with a weak body. Exercise is beneficial for us, Mary." Miss Elizabeth flashed her sister a kindly smile, revealing lips the color of strawberry preserves.

The youngest girls splashed Miss Mary, reminding me to blink and look elsewhere.

"Perhaps Mary would enjoy swimming more if you did not splash her so much, Lydia." Miss Bennet's gentle voice calmed them by a degree.

The other giggly daughter, Miss Kitty, suddenly jumped. "Something just brushed over my foot!"

"Stop whinging, you ninny! It is probably only a fish or a water reed." Miss Lydia's lack of sympathy confirmed her immaturity. She could not be older than Georgiana, but her lack of the education a gently-bred young lady ought to possess was apparent. I presumed this was yet another example of her father's negligence.

Miss Bennet's forbearing sigh was nearly imperceptible—I only saw it because I had almost exhausted my supply of bread and felt I must avoid looking at Miss Elizabeth now that I had noticed her lips were the same color as my favorite fruit. What was it about her that captivated me so? She was handsome, but not *that* handsome. She was daring, but I ought not to admire that.

"Do you know how to swim, Mr. Bingley?" Miss Bennet asked, deftly steering the conversation and attention away from her younger sisters.

"Indeed, I do, though not as well as Darcy."

Again, all eyes turned to me. I wished Bingley would quit praising me.

"And is Miss Bingley so accomplished?" Miss Elizabeth graciously turned the topic away from me and challenged that lady's earlier comment.

"Hardly!" Miss Bingley sniffed.

Miss Bennet replied with a kindness Miss Bingley did not deserve. "The bank along your side of the stream slopes more gently into the water than it does on this side. You may wade safely there. Only take care not to get too close to the center where the water is deepest."

She continued speaking before Miss Bingley could utter another insult. "You are a strong swimmer, Mr. Darcy?"

I tried to look at her without staring. "Yes. My estate has many ponds and lakes." My voice came out smoothly, and I was inordinately pleased with myself.

"In Derbyshire, Mr. Bingley said? Does it ever get warm enough to swim there?"

"It does, though not like this." Again, smooth.

"Yes, this is extraordinary weather. Early planters will have lost their seed, I fear."

What an unusual—and insightful—observation for a young lady to make! Not wishing to ruin my eloquence, I tossed the last of the bread into the stream for the happy duck to dive after.

"She has taken a fancy to you." I heard the smile in Miss Elizabeth's voice. This time, she was not laughing at me but with me.

A dangerously heady sensation seized me with this evidence that I had pleased her. My initial reaction was to determine henceforth to fill my pockets with crumbs so that she might always see me feeding the ducks. But that was foolish, and I no sooner thought it than I disregarded the notion. Who was Miss Elizabeth to me that I should seek her approval?

"An honor, to be sure," Richard teased.

"Oh, but ducks are exceptional judges of character. Did you not know that, *Colonel*?" Miss Lydia emphasized his rank, making it plain that she had set her cap at him. She was the sort to pursue any man with a red coat.

Miss Kitty added, "Every regiment and garrison should have a raft of ducks to detect spies and traitors."

Their comments, while silly, were an improvement

over their earlier vulgar displays. I recognized what a challenge it must be for the older Bennet sisters to manage two such girls without the backing of their father.

Their mother could be no better. In fairness, I attempted to reserve judgment until I could observe the matron... whenever that might be. Did she favor her eldest daughters or the youngest? "Do you often come here?" My gaze settled upon Miss Elizabeth with my usual confidence.

Miss Bingley rode closer to me, interrupting my tête-à-tête with the dangerous water nymph. "If you would be so kind to assist me down, Mr. Darcy?"

Brushing the crumbs from my hands, I handed her down, partly grateful for the distraction. It would ultimately be unkind for me to single Miss Elizabeth out in my attentions. We were from different spheres and could have little in common beyond this stream.

The duck hissed and flapped her wings.

"Jemima!" Miss Elizabeth chastised, slipping into the water and swimming closer to the offended fowl.

"The duck is named Jemima?" Richard turned toward the disturbance.

Miss Mary explained, "It is a biblical name. One of Job's daughters was named Jemima."

"She was one of the most beautiful women in the land," proclaimed Miss Kitty.

"...for her virtue as much as for her appearance," countered Miss Mary.

Jemima hissed again, her beady eyes trained on Miss Bingley.

Miss Elizabeth, now within an arm's reach of Jemima, looked between the duck and the damsel. "Miss Bingley, I pray you, do not come any closer."

"Me, afraid of a docile duck?" Miss Bingley scoffed. "Really!" She stepped forward and reached for my arm.

Quicker than the flick of her tail, Jemima swam out of Miss Elizabeth's reach to the riverbank, neck stretched out and running as fast as her webbed feet could carry her—directly at Miss Bingley.

"Get it away!" the lady yelped.

Stepping lightly so as not to hurt the duck, I hefted Miss Bingley back onto her saddle and out of the reach of the furious fowl, who snapped at her skirts.

Miss Bingley huffed, her complexion deepening to an unbecoming shade. Her eyes narrowed as they fixed on something directly behind me.

When I turned, there stood Miss Elizabeth on the bank, water streaming down her shapely ankles and dripping on her bare feet. She was wet from head to toe, and her nearness made me feel like a kettle about to boil. I forced my eyes up and beheld the lady up close. Her face was as handsome as her form. I looked down at my sleeve, expecting to see vapor rising off my person.

The duck wiggled in her arms. Miss Elizabeth held Jemima with firm hands, nuzzling the riled duck's head down and tucking it into the crook of her arm, away from the offensive Miss Bingley.

"You naughty girl! You will scare off our new neighbors, and then who will feed you crumbs from their pockets? You did not think of that, did you, you silly duck?" Speaking to it softly, she walked into the stream and set Jemima on the glassy surface, then stood between the duck and Miss Bingley, who sat haughtily atop her horse.

A strong and utterly inappropriate urge to laugh seized me, and I coughed into my arm to suppress it. When Miss Elizabeth's eyes met mine with a glee matching my own, I thought my ribs would bruise with the effort it took to restrain my amusement.

Chapter Six

"Well, I would never—" Miss Bingley blustered up the embankment and down the other side, away from the stream and our new acquaintances.

"Never what? Offend a duck?" Richard spoke in a droll tone that tested my waning restraint.

Miss Bingley jutted out her chin. "Dreadful creature."

She did not specify who the dreadful creature was —Richard or the duck. I sucked in a much-needed breath, wondering how long I could hold burgeoning laughter before I burst.

"Jemima is a duck of firm opinions—an admirable trait, in my opinion," Richard observed with faux solemnity.

I bit my lips together and sucked in my breath.

Bingley shook his head. "What did you do to the poor duck to turn her against you, Caro?"

His sister's nostrils flared. "I would not be surprised if that rustic hoyden had something to do with it."

"A trained duck?" I said in a strained whisper, forcing my face into a mask of indifference, but not before Richard caught my lips twitching. My strength was not equal to my resolve. I did not know how much longer I could maintain my composure.

"One must cast a wary eye on these modern country maidens." Richard's tone was too grave to be taken seriously. "First, they have the audacity to swim expertly, and now we learn that they are accomplished duck handlers. What will they think of next?"

This was too much. A barkish laugh ripped from my chest. Pure mirth swelled in my eyes and blurred my vision. Richard guffawed beside me, and Bingley soon joined us. The three of us ignored the fuming glares of a woman whose absurd reasoning only added to the hilarity of the moment.

My stomach ached and my cheeks pinched, but now that the dam had burst, I found it difficult to temper my humor.

"It was terribly improper of her to get out of the water with gentlemen present," Miss Bingley insisted. "Her feet were bare."

Good thing she had been riding behind me and

was spared the indecency of seeing Miss Elizabeth's bare calves.

Never before had I pondered the appeal of a woman's lowest extremities. I was hardly a connoisseur, but Miss Elizabeth's slender feet—her dainty toes tipped with clean, white nails—seemed remarkably fine to me. I could not laugh at them. I brushed the tears of merriment from my face.

"That entire family is dreadfully scandalous! I would never swim where I might be seen by anyone passing by." Miss Bingley looked about for support but found none.

"Caroline," Bingley said in a sterner tone, "the Bennets had no way of knowing anyone would see them. Netherfield Park has been empty for years, and there is nobody else nearby to chance upon them. It is perfectly proper for them to swim on their own property."

"In a stream they share with you! It is your property, too, and as you are an unattached gentleman, they ought to take more care. You will need to be cautious lest one of them attempts to trap you into an unequal union."

"Unequal? They are daughters of landed gentry! As such, they are our superiors."

"Their conduct suggests they do not hold themselves to the same standards a gentlewoman does."

"You have no idea how tempted I was to join them in the water!"

"You would not dare! Mr. Darcy would never stoop to such a desperate measure. Did you not see how he hardly spoke to them?"

That was not at all what had happened. Yes, initially I was regrettably silent, but that had nothing to do with expressing my disapproval and everything to do with my embarrassment.

"Darcy is always quiet among new acquaintances! That is his way." Bingley defended me masterfully.

Miss Bingley rolled her eyes. "You would do well to listen to me, Charles. I am right. There is nothing more undignified than being caught bathing... and by strangers! I have never met a more impertinent female than that Miss Elizabeth."

Neither had I. I ought to have disapproved as Miss Bingley did, yet I found myself subduing another smile at the recollection.

"She splashed Mr. Darcy!"

I had heard enough of Miss Bingley's complaints against a young lady whose playful disposition and frank humor were as refreshing as the water with which she had splashed me. "A kindness for which I am indebted."

Richard smirked. "I wish she might have splashed me!"

Miss Bingley continued, too vexed to comprehend that her complaints were in direct opposition to my compliment. "And her hair! A tangled, snarled nest! I pity her poor maid."

Ah, yes—slick, dark curls trailing down her back to her waist. I imagined Miss Elizabeth's hair splayed around her face, lightened by the sun while it dried, her curls wild and untamable. Much like the lady herself, I surmised.

Miss Bingley tittered cruelly. "Oh, my. Given the state of her bedraggled coiffure, I doubt she has a maid!"

What she could not know was that her comments only fueled my curiosity and strengthened my inclination toward Miss Elizabeth.

Brow furrowed, Bingley looked at me with his mouth agape. I merely returned his look. It was *his* place to correct his sister, not mine.

"Out with it, man!" Richard urged.

Chest out, hands clenched, Bingley said, "Caroline, you are being churlish."

"Nonsense, Charles. I merely speak the truth."

"And?" Richard prompted, motioning with his hand for Bingley to continue.

"And... it is most unbecoming." Bingley uttered this as firmly as I had ever heard him. In Bingley's mind, it was a scathing chastisement.

Miss Bingley dismissed his correction. He was wrong; she was right. That was that, in her narrow mind.

One look at Richard's dissatisfied expression was enough to make me hold my breath yet again and clutch my poor, aching ribs.

By the time we returned to Netherfield, I was in a lamentable state. Between the miserable sun and the flashes of Miss Elizabeth's brilliant smile and clinging flannel, I needed a cold bath. For heaven's sake, this was England, not the tropical climes near the equator! The sticky weather could not last forever, though I could hardly remember the last time it had rained.

My bath gave only temporary relief. It was too hot to drink tea, too hot to sleep. Too hot to do anything but sit motionless with one's thoughts.

The bedsheets stuck to my body. My dreams provided both respite and torment; they were filled with pools of cool water surrounded by a copse of trees and an intrepid young lady flying through the air from a rope, laughing.

Chapter Seven

I kicked free of the suffocating coverlets the following morning and donned my lightest garments, which were still grievously excessive. Then I made my way out to the hall in search of Richard and Bingley.

Richard's years in the army had turned him into an early riser, and I found him easily enough. Together we took on the task of waking Bingley, who suffered dearly whenever he was made to wake before breakfast. But if we were to escape unnoticed, we had precious little time to waste.

I knocked lightly, hoping at least to get the attention of his valet without rousing the rest of the household.

Richard pressed his ear against the door, stepping away just a moment before the barrier opened. Bingley stood there, his boots dangling from one hand. He looked up and down the hall guiltily, appearing in all respects like a schoolboy sneaking out of his dormitory. "I had thought to inspect that swimming spot Mr. Bennet told us about yesterday before breaking my fast," he whispered.

"We are of a united purpose," I gravely assured him.

"Good. Only I beg you not to say a word to Caroline or I shall never hear the end of it."

Being an easy promise to make, Richard and I nodded our agreement. Together, the three of us strode outdoors to the stables under the warming sun.

The place Mr. Bennet had indicated was not difficult to find. It did not boast a large oak with a rope swing, but the river was wider and the current calmer, providing a peaceful oasis for the otters and ducks we had been told we would find.

As I stripped down to the cotton summer trousers I had wiggled my doeskin breeches over (to Weller's silent but unmistakable protests), I kept a watchful eye out for Jemima, having made certain to save a piece of bread for her on the chance she might swim our way.

The taller the mound of garments on the grass grew, the more deeply I could breathe and the greater I could appreciate my surroundings. A light breeze tickled my skin.

Bingley stepped into the water, stopping when his feet were submerged no higher than his ankles. "It is colder than I thought it would be." He shivered.

Perfect. I nodded at Richard, who already squinted at the surface searching for dangerous obstacles lurking below. The picture of a man idly biding his time.

I did not need him to count down from three aloud to know that this was a race. It was always a race. A race I had always won and would continue to win as long as I drew breath.

Three. Two.

"One!" Richard bellowed just as I sprang forward. We ran into the water, my longer strides giving me the advantage until the water deepened enough to resist me. I plunged forward, diving into the cool depth at the middle of the river. A jolt of chill chattered in my chin, but I pressed on, one arm over the other, swimming upstream until my blood warmed and my breath came in labored gasps.

Flipping around, using my hands to stay afloat, I saw Richard only two lengths behind me.

Bingley still stood ankle-deep at the edge of the river, shivering. Richard shook his head, just as I am certain I did. That would not do. Bingley was an excellent swimmer—I ought to know because I was the one who taught him ages ago at Eton—but he invariably took an eternity to muster up the courage to take the plunge.

Now that I thought about it, he was hesitant in many more ways than in his swimming...

Perhaps it was an impulse from my youth or the memory of playful Miss Elizabeth, but before I thought my action through to completion, I had returned to him downstream, formed scoops with my hands, and heaved as much water as I could hold onto Bingley. Never one to miss out on the fun, Richard soon joined me.

Bingley was too stunned to make a noise at first. He stood in place, dripping, jaw dropped to his chest. "I cannot believe you did that."

I filled my hands with water. "If Bingley will not come to the river, then the river must come to Bingley."

"Hey, you have that backwards!" Bingley protested.

I shrugged. "Does it matter? You have not moved an inch, and yet you are just as wet as if you had swum."

Richard added, "The longer you stand there, the redder your sunburn will be."

That was all the encouragement Bingley required.

We raced up and down the river until our fingers wrinkled.

Pulling tight breeches over damp skin was no easy feat. By the time I had accomplished this, I was sweaty enough to merit another swim. The day had grown considerably hotter. I glared at my linen shirt with its high collars. I fumbled with the impossibly minuscule buttons on my waistcoat—all eleven of them—but it was the cravat which inspired a heaving sigh.

"Feels like a noose." Richard grimaced as he prepared to don his own neck cloth.

Bingley shrugged and draped his around his neck, not bothering to tie it. Considering the circumstances, I considered it the perfect solution.

The groom held our horses in the shade of a thicket a touch downstream.

It was there—that much closer to the same spot where I had first seen Miss Elizabeth the day before—that I heard her laugh. I shook my head, trying to dispel myself of the sound, but it only became stronger. Concluding that I must have water in my ear, I cocked my head to the side and shook my earlobe. Miss Elizabeth had been ever present in my thoughts, and now it would seem that she was a consistent resonance in my ears.

Richard's eyebrows bunched together in a deep V. "Are you quite well, Darcy?"

Dropping my hand from my ringing ear, I stood erect. "Of course," I answered a touch too testily and inwardly cringed. Had I reacted more indifferently, Richard would have dropped the matter. Not now.

A stupid grin spread over his lips. "Hearing things, are you, old man?"

Richard laughed at us both as Bingley stood still and listened. "I hear it, too! From downstream! It must be the Bennets." Richard's laughter died, and he, too, stood still and strained his ear.

The sound I had thought was in my head was very real. The realization that Richard had not heard it at all gave me all the ammunition I needed, and I clapped him on the shoulder. "Not hearing like you used to, old man?" To smile now would have been petty, so I restrained myself... until I turned to mount my horse.

"They are a contented lot." Bingley pulled himself onto his steed. "I can imagine no pleasanter way of spending my day than with my family, watching them enjoy the river during a hot spell."

I knew where his reasoning was leading. To be truthful, I had hoped to avoid the Bennets entirely... while also secretly wishing that I might catch just one more glimpse of Miss Elizabeth. Now that the opportunity was here, I did not trust myself *not* to stare at the young lady who, unbidden, appeared too often in my thoughts.

As I expected, Bingley finally suggested that we ride downstream to exchange a pleasant word with his new neighbors. How weak my resolution was—I could not summon even one objection! My desire to see Miss Elizabeth far outweighed the danger I sensed she presented to me.

Childish squeals grew louder as we rounded the bend that opened to calm waters. This time, there were children—three of them. Miss Elizabeth had her arms wrapped around a small girl who buried her face in Miss Elizabeth's neck and clung onto her hair while two boys jumped and splashed around them.

Miss Elizabeth deftly scooped a handful of water with her free hand and generously doused the boys, much to their delight.

A man perched on the same root Mr. Bennet had been sitting upon the day before, his collar unbuttoned and his feet in the water. A woman wearing a dark flannel from neck to toes came around the tree. "Jamie, Charlie, settle down and let Auntie Lizzy teach Esther to swim."

The man noticed us first. Raising his hand, he greeted us with a friendly tone. "Good morning to you, sirs! It is a fine day by the stream, is it not?"

Miss Elizabeth twirled around, her arms still holding the little girl. Her eyes met mine. As her smile widened, so did the swelling sensation in my chest. I squelched that response with a cold dash of reality. Too many women of the *ton* had attempted to appeal to my vanity and draw my attention...

Thus began an argument between my head and my heart. *Too many women have tried to turn your head,* I reasoned. *She is different,* my heart whispered back.

Was Miss Elizabeth like all the other ladies? So far, she had been nothing like them.

Then why am I so quick to judge her with them? All she had done was smile. And it was a sincere smile. There had been nothing calculating in it, just pure joy. Joy at seeing *me*.

My chest resumed swelling again. It disturbed me to find that I had followed my own reasoning right back where I had started. I already knew the dangers of trusting my heart, but now I had to exercise extra caution with my mind as well! *Traitor.*

I looked purposefully away from her to the man and woman now sitting together at the base of the oak.

If Miss Elizabeth noticed my discomfiture, she gracefully smoothed over it when she performed introductions. "Mr. Darcy, Colonel Fitzwilliam, Mr. Bingley, pray allow me to introduce my uncle, Mr. Edward Gardiner, and my aunt, Mrs. Madeline Gardiner, of Gracechurch Street in London."

"My grandfather had warehouses on Gracechurch Street!" Bingley said.

Mr. Gardiner chuckled. "Then you know how wretched the river smells right now!"

"It is horrible on a good day," Bingley agreed. "How convenient for you to have relatives with a country estate only half of a day's ride away."

The Gardiners nodded enthusiastically. Miss Elizabeth favored them with an affectionate smile. "You are welcome to visit anytime—wretched, reeking river or not." She then introduced my group more completely. My soft brain responded to the pleasant sound of "Pemberley" on Miss Elizabeth's tongue but jolted to attention when Mrs. Gardiner gasped.

"Pemberley, you say? What a lovely coincidence! I hail from Lambton."

I looked at the aunt more closely—she was pleasantly plump, her dark hair softened by the warmth in her eyes. Just like my mother's. The tenderness with which she regarded her children and the respect with which she looked at her husband gripped my heart. That kind of love was rare.

"Mr. Gardiner knows what a sacrifice it was for me to leave Lambton," she said, "although he has made our home a happy one, and I have many pleasant memories of my childhood home."

She shifted her gaze from her husband to the boy by Miss Elizabeth, and then she looked over at the water. Struggling up from her perch, her eyes darted wildly over the river with her hand at her throat. "Where is Jamie?" Louder, she called, "Jamie?!"

Miss Elizabeth immediately pointed to a spot under her aunt's feet. "He is hiding under the tree roots, Aunt. Jamie, come out from there. Your mother is worried."

The boy emerged from his hiding spot. "I did not mean to startle you, Mama! It is the perfect spot to hide from pirates."

"One must be prepared for such an occurrence." His father nodded gravely.

"It is the best spot! I could see them, but they could not see me!"

Richard said, "It is a fine place to bury a treasure. You do not suppose the oak roots conceal a chest of Spanish doubloons, do you, lad?"

Miss Elizabeth, now holding her niece on her hip, sent a trail of water splashing in Jamie's direction. "Let us be grateful that none of these gentlemen are pirates, then." Her eyes widened, and she dropped her voice theatrically as she turned to us. "You are not pirates, are you, sirs?"

She was charming, and I found myself as tongue-tied as I had been the day before.

The children laughed, and Charlie climbed up the roots with the rope swing in his hand. Standing at the top, he considered climbing higher up the base of the tree. Evidently, he decided the root was enough to test his courage. With a whoop to make certain all eyes were upon him, he jumped and swung over the water, landing with a brilliant splash in the middle of the river.

He paddled closer to the shore, gaining his footing and pumping his arms in the air. "I did it!"

Jamie stuck his tongue out at his older brother. "Auntie Lizzy does it better!"

Miss Elizabeth laughed tensely. "When both of you have as much practice as I have had, you will both exceed my nominal skill, I assure you."

Charlie bobbed up and down. "Will you teach us?"

There was a redness in her face that had not been there before. "Perhaps later."

Was she embarrassed? She should not be. Miss Bingley was not here to take offense. And the laws of physics prevented her from stopping mid-swing. She could not help that I, an unrelated gentleman, had seen her legs.

"Please?" Both boys continued to plead.

"Later." She glanced briefly in our direction and then back to her nephews.

I understood her hesitation. Just as I had cast her with all the ladies of the *ton*, so she could easily group us with the pretentious gentlemen of the upper crust. A lady of quality was expected to exhibit her talents on the instrument or with her paints. To display any skill which might expose an ankle or prove strength beyond the ability to lift a teapot would certainly be frowned upon—and all the more so with three gentlemen present!

I wished I could dispel her of this prejudiced notion. Until she understood our characters better, she would refrain from playing with her nephews as they wished until we departed. We were spoiling the children's fun... Miss Elizabeth's fun. There was nothing to do but take our leave.

As we rode away, I heard a joyous laugh and a large splash. I resisted the urge to turn around, telling myself that the trees and bushes would block my view, anyway.

And that is exactly what I saw when I turned. Nothing but branches and thickets... and that lovely sound that trilled in my ears and curled my lips upward.

Chapter Eight

Three mornings passed. On every one, Richard, Bingley, and I went to the river. Each day my anticipation built with the yearning to hear the merrymaking from Longbourn's residents and guests. And every day, I was disappointed to hear no sound other than rippling water and fluttering leaves.

Bingley sighed. "Perhaps we shall chance upon them on the morrow."

"The weather is about to break. I feel it in my bones," Richard said.

"Suffering from rheumatism already?" I attempted to hide my own disgruntlement. If this unusually hot weather ceased, so would our daily trips to the stream. Where else could I chance upon Miss Elizabeth again?

The water was cool, but it did not feel as refreshing as it had that first day. Several times, I caught myself looking down the river, my humor becoming more sullen in the absence of her laughter.

Bingley and Richard must have felt it too, for we did not swim long. Somehow, we ended up riding past the giant oak tree on our way back to Netherfield.

I tried to appear indifferent when nobody was there. Why should I wish to see Miss Elizabeth? We had hardly spoken. I had no reason to believe I had given her a favorable impression of my character with my silence and failed attempt to save a lady who did not need saving.

I considered whether I might come up with a rational reason to call at Longbourn, but the heat was as adept at keeping families indoors as was a downpour of rain. Unless one's destination was a stream, to venture out of doors was to invite misery; to call elsewhere would be to impose misery on another.

My heart had leaped in my chest when Bingley had suggested an outdoor picnic and then promptly plummeted to its proper place when it was unanimously agreed that not even the shadiest spot would provide enough relief for everyone in our party. Not to mention that flies thrived in this weather.

And so we settled in the billiard room, wishing that we were elsewhere and in better company than we were presently.

My hair was not completely dry when the butler appeared in the doorway. He cleared his throat and dabbed his forehead with a handkerchief. "You have callers in the parlor, sir."

Callers? Only one lacking sense would call in this weather. I set down my cue, all attention.

"Sir William Lucas and his son. I could not rightly make them wait for a reply—"

"Of course not, Pratt. You acted as I would have directed, had you asked. In the future, I hope you show all our callers into the parlor as you did today."

I bit my lips together at Bingley's naivety. He would learn soon enough that not all callers are equally welcome.

I sighed and reached for the queue to take a shot, struggling to understand the depth of my displeasure. Miss Elizabeth did not lack sense; I could hardly expect her to call when her good judgment would keep her either indoors or at the stream.

"Shall I tell Sir William you are in?" Pratt asked, still having received no clear command from his master.

"Oh! Yes, of course. I shall be down directly."

More to prove my indifference to my snickering cousin than to convey any particular interest in Netherfield's neighbors, I accompanied Bingley to the parlor.

Sir William was a rotund man with cheeks that I suspected were perpetually ruddy. Although he favored lofty words and spoke a great deal of utter nonsense, his manners were so unassuming and pleasant that I could not take offense at him. He clearly sought to better his position in the world and expounded at length upon his one experience at St. James. But instead of presuming that his knighthood entitled him to belong to the higher circles, he appeared in awe that he was actually permitted to mingle with them. Senseless but unassuming. An intriguing combination—and for certain, a rare one.

His son nodded eagerly but said little. If his dress was an outer expression of his inner qualities, then I was grateful for his silence. Such a startling combination of yellow and green!

Mrs. Hurst and Miss Bingley exchanged haughty glances, but Mr. Lucas' waistcoat did not evaporate under their scrutiny. Nor did Sir William alter his manner. He was confidently awestruck, which suited his hostesses well enough.

Finally, after lengthy introductions and aimless chatter, Sir William stated the reason for his call. "I apologize for the early hour of my call, but I had hoped to return to Lucas Lodge before the heat became overbearing. It was most kind of you to allow me to wait for you in the parlor! I suppose I ought not to be surprised —you *are* a gentleman welcomed in the first circles. I would not have ventured to call at all had I not felt it imperative to inform you of the next public assembly to be held in Meryton. Your neighbors are desirous of your company and wish to extend to you and your household a warm welcome."

There were few things more miserable than a night of dancing in a crowded room that reeked of sweat and heavy perfume. But Miss Elizabeth seemed like a lady who would enjoy dancing and conversation. Was she as adept at dancing as she was at swimming and acrobatics? I would forgo silk for cooler linen if the weather did not break before the night of the assembly. Not even Weller would argue, given the unbearable heat of the past week.

I looked through the window glass at the sky. Was that a sliver of gray on the horizon? I could only pray that it was!

Sir William followed my glance. With a chuckle, he pulled a wilted handkerchief out of his pocket and wiped it over his face. "I noticed some clouds on the drive here. Perhaps the storm will break before the assembly next week."

"We look forward to it!" Bingley assured him with enthusiasm.

Once Pratt had seen Sir William and his son out, Miss Bingley rolled her eyes. "How dreadful to have to mingle with the locals."

Bingley's brows furrowed. "There are several families of quality who plan to attend." He had made certain the Bennets would be there. While Sir William had expressed doubt about Mr. Bennet making an appearance, he had assured them that Mrs. Bennet and her five daughters would certainly be in attendance.

"Of course they will be there! With five daughters

to marry off, they will wish to snag a wealthy bachelor." Miss Bingley spoke between the flutters of her fan. "Take care and keep your distance, Charles."

"What can you know of them, Caroline? You speak of them as if they were looking to marry a fortune."

Most people *did* marry for a fortune, but I kept the thought to myself.

"And are they not?" Miss Bingley scoffed spitefully. "I have learned from impeccable sources that none of the girls have a dowry worth mentioning. Their father allows them to read extensively from his library but has never employed a governess to see to their education. They do not have a tutor, nor have they gone to town to study under masters. They have few accomplishments."

"If they have any at all!" added Mrs. Hurst.

"Such woeful negligence. Any gentleman who wished to attach himself to such a family would live to regret it. If you do not wish to be brought to absolute ruin, you will listen to me, Charles, and give the Bennets no more attention than you would to a shop-keeper's plain daughter."

My stomach turned sour. I wanted so badly to deny her assertions, but I could not deny what was likely true. The claims against Mr. Bennet aligned with my own observations, and the silliness of his youngest offspring was the added proof.

However, I would bet my favorite horse that Miss Elizabeth had made good use of her father's library.

And there was no fault to find in her eldest sister's conduct. Both of them had risen above circumstances which would have squashed the spirit of a lady with less initiative. Did not such a disposition deserve praise? I opened my mouth to say as much, but the topic had already veered in another direction.

"They might as well be farmers for all the fashion we have seen since we left London." Mrs. Hurst spoke confidently despite how little of Meryton society she had seen thus far. At least the Bennets were no longer the sole target of her contempt.

Miss Bingley fanned her face. "It falls to us to display the latest fashions for them." With that, the two leaned closer together on the settee plotting their grand debut into a society they scorned.

Mrs. Hurst addressed her husband. "I shall have a word with your valet to see about coordinating our attire. My blue gown suits me best, and you have a matching silk waistcoat."

"Silk? In this heat?" he complained. She continued planning without pause, showing no consideration for his comfort.

"What color waistcoat will you wear, Mr. Darcy?" Miss Bingley smiled at me coyly.

I would have chosen to don livery rather than match Miss Bingley at the Meryton Assembly. "Whatever Weller deems suitable," I answered in a bland tone.

"I shall have my maid consult with your valet," she

responded, undeterred. *That* was a conversation I would have liked to witness. Weller had attended to royalty in Vienna before the war and his return to England. He was renowned for his high standards and staunchness in maintaining them. Neither Miss Bingley nor her maid would succeed in prying information from him.

Bingley's sisters had set themselves upon a mission to demonstrate their superiority through the quality of their silk gowns and their fashionably complex coiffures. They believed they would awe their neighbors by humiliating them. If the temperatures held, their own discomfort would be a harsh punishment for their pride—though I also wished that Miss Bingley might swoon in the arms of one of the farmers she so disdained.

While I was in the midst of these mischievous thoughts, Mr. Hurst sought to change the topic of discourse. He turned to his brother-in-law. "Where were you this morning?"

Bingley blanched. He soon gathered himself to answer, knowing full well what consequences he would face. "I went swimming in the stream."

Twin gasps erupted from the settee. Bingley turned to face his sisters, resignation writ in his expression.

"I went with him." Richard ensured that he would get his fair share of the ladies' disapproval, thus lessening Bingley's portion.

"As did I." I nodded at my partners in crime, the effort not to smile intensifying as Miss Bingley struggled to contain her shock. She could not chastise her brother without including me and Richard. The consternation on her face was amusing to watch.

What would she think if I attempted to flip from the rope swing just as Miss Elizabeth had done? *Shocking! Highly improper! A highborn gentleman would never stoop to such a base trick!* Her imagined arguments fueled the flame of my intention until it burned within me.

That swing had awakened pleasant memories of my youth, stirring that carefree daredevil within who challenged me to prove I had not turned into a boorish ninny incapable of a trifling flip from a rope.

With vastly improved spirits, I returned to the stuffy billiard room and planned my rebellion.

Chapter Nine

I awoke at dawn. Eagerness made my ablutions clumsier than usual, but I refused to wake my valet. Taking a cue from Bingley, I carried my boots downstairs, testing each step with the tips of my stockinged toes. Bingley would require too much explanation; Richard would tease me mercilessly—I would spare myself both conversations by going alone.

As I wriggled my feet into the boots and crossed the yard to the stables, my conviction in the wisdom of my decision strengthened. The air was heavier that morning than it had been previously. There was a charge to it that made the hair on my arms stand on end. A storm was brewing. If I was to have a go at the rope swing, it was now or never.

Not a soul was in sight as I rode to the stream. It was perfect.

Tying my horse to a sturdy branch, I scanned the

area. Not even Jemima appeared. Leaving the day-old bread Cook had saved for me in my saddlebag, I stripped down to my drawers in seconds. I did not have the luxury of time on my side; if I was to achieve my feat before Richard noticed I was gone, I must hurry.

Charging into the water and past the shock of the cold, I swam to the middle of the stream where the rope dangled over the surface. Line in hand, I swam over to the oak tree and climbed up the root. Water ran down my skin, leaving a trail of gooseflesh in its wake. I shivered and clutched onto the rope with both hands. Leaning forward, I tested my weight against the branch. It would hold.

Satisfied, I climbed as far up the trunk as my wet feet on the slick surface allowed. Then I tightened my grip and jumped.

Up, up, up I flew, blazing a path through the air, tears tugging at the corners of my eyes, cheeks tight with a grin. It was exhilarating! I let out a triumphant whoop and waited for the weightlessness at the top.

Almost there... almost there... now! I tipped backwards, ready to release my hold on the rope.

SNAP!

The rope went slack in my hands. I flailed in the air, smacking inelegantly—and rather painfully—against the water.

A split second before the rest of me dunked under the surface, I heard a high-pitched yelp. It had not come from me. As startled as I was, there was nothing womanly about my scream.

My eyes opened underwater, but I saw nothing except for two approaching duck feet. Jemima? That outcry was not from her, either. Who did it belong to?

I swam closer to Netherfield's half of the shore until my feet gained the ground, but there I stopped. Only my head was above the surface. "Who is there? Show yourself!" I demanded.

Miss Elizabeth and an older woman I had not yet met emerged from under the same root the Gardiner boy had disappeared under days before. The older woman's hair was piled in a pasty mess on top of her head. She was still handsome.

This must be Mrs. Bennet. While Miss Elizabeth's hair was darker, there was no mistaking the resemblance to her mother. Two ladies. Two ladies who had seen me in naught but my wet summer drawers.

My ire increased. "Why did you not make your presence known?!" A gentleman never shouts at a lady, but I came perilously close to doing just that.

Raising her chin, Miss Elizabeth replied saucily. "And why were you on our side of the river? Is upstream—where my father encouraged you to swim at your leisure with complete privacy—not good enough for you that you had to intrude on our property?"

I followed her gaze to the frayed remains of the rope. My anger subsided. Not only had I trespassed, but I had damaged their property. My contrition tempered my tone, but I noted that she had not answered my question. "My apologies. I will make reparations before the end of the day. Now why did you not alert me to your presence?"

Mrs. Bennet beamed. "How charming and responsible!" She elbowed her daughter (I could not see the gesture but, given her movement and the consequential wince from her daughter, I inferred as much.) "And so handsomely—"

"Mama! You have not yet met the guest of our newest neighbor at Netherfield Park." She rushed through introductions.

I only half paid attention, as I had to wonder with increasing horror just how much Mrs. Bennet had seen. Dear Lord, I had walked directly over them in wet drawers! I might as well have pranced about them naked!

I felt ill. The way Mrs. Bennet smiled at me with sharp eyes did little to ease the tumult twisting in my stomach.

Miss Elizabeth continued, "Mr. Darcy, pray allow me to assure you that it was modesty which prevented us from calling out."

"Modesty?! You could not have seen me in a more immodest state!" My entire self burned so hot, I was surprised that no steam rose around me.

"I swear on my father's name that I saw nothing," Miss Elizabeth countered with a passionate tremor.

Her mother said nothing, and one squelching look

from her daughter prevented her from saying anything at all. She continued, "Pray hear me, sir, and I shall explain. My mother cannot swim. Since the weather is about to change, she asked me to help her bathe and wash her hair before the children wake. Today is their last opportunity to play at the river, so we came early to allow them more time. I must have been scrubbing my mother's hair when you first arrived. When I did finally see you... you began disrobing... and I... I panicked."

Was this how spontaneous combustion happened? I expected to burst into flames any second. I ran my wet hands over my face as I listened to every horrific word.

"I turned my back, but you were so quick! I heard you enter the water before I could think to speak up. When I heard the rope creak, I assumed you would attempt some trick, after which you would continue on your way without any trouble from us. So we waited in silence."

The top of her shift stuck to her shoulders, as transparent as my drawers. Her arms were crossed in front of her. She had not been speaking of my modesty, but of her own and her mother's.

"You saw nothing?"

"No, I did not."

I believed Miss Elizabeth when she said that she had seen nothing. Perhaps Mrs. Bennet had not either? I had to hope. All the bluster departed from me in one deep exhale. Her explanation was perfectly reasonable. I felt like a brute for shouting at her. "Pray accept my apology for the intrusion. I assumed nobody would be here."

"Yes, well, you know what assuming does, do you not?"

My gasp might have turned into a laugh had I not choked. Did she really just imply that I was a fool? A donkey? To my face? Not since my father's death had anyone dared speak to me so bluntly... except for Richard. I replied to her, just as I had done many times to my father. "It takes one to know one."

...At which she flashed her teeth and laughed. My heart flopped in my chest, because that was exactly how my father had always reacted. Mama would scold us both and pretend to be appalled, but her eyes sparkled just as Miss Elizabeth's did.

"Lizzy! Do not offend the gentleman, or he will never make you an offer!" Mrs. Bennet slapped a chunk of hair away from her face. Her statement ought to have offended me, but after my failed trick, I was inclined to overlook her brashness.

"Nonsense, Mama. Mr. Darcy has no interest whatsoever in me."

Now who was assuming? I was not hearing wedding bells or smelling orange blossoms, but Miss Elizabeth had most certainly piqued my interest.

She looked at me for confirmation. Instead of lying, I changed the subject. "If you would both be so kind, I must somehow exit the water to retrieve my clothing and untie my horse." *Oh, what I would give for a groom right now!*

Miss Elizabeth colored and instantly turned around. Mrs. Bennet watched me until her daughter apparently jabbed her in the ribs. "What? He has nothing I have not seen—"

"Mama!"

If our brief encounter this morning was a fair indicator, I had the impression that Miss Elizabeth most often addressed her mother with some level of contrition or embarrassment.

"I beg you to acquiesce, Mama. We are at a standstill, and Mr. Darcy is trusting us to act honorably. Or would you prefer that we keep our shoulders below the water all day until someone comes along to fetch his clothing for him or ours for us?"

Mrs. Bennet shrugged. "It would give you time to converse and get to know each other better."

"Not every conversation leads to a courtship, Mama."

Mrs. Bennet fervently disagreed. She was in no hurry to turn, and I would not move an inch up the bank until she did. Aside from wondering how much of me she had seen, I now had to worry about how much trouble she would cause about today's incident.

Miss Elizabeth's lips thinned, and her nostrils flared. "If you agree to not only turn your back to allow Mr. Darcy the privacy required to dress and leave without causing further embarrassment but also to never speak a word of what has happened today—"

"Not even to my sister?" Mrs. Bennet pouted.

"Especially not to Aunt Philips! Not to Lady Lucas, and certainly not to Lydia, or to anyone else you might be tempted to tell. Not a word! Do you understand?"

Mrs. Bennet's lips twisted.

"I shall give you my pin money for this month to do with as you please," Miss Elizabeth offered.

"And next month's?"

"Very well."

Mrs. Bennet had gained the upper hand, as she was aware. She wet her lips and rubbed her hands together. "You will also agree to help Sara with the entire household's mending so it is ready before the assembly. *And* you will wear the gown and coiffure I choose for the ball."

Miss Elizabeth spoke through gritted teeth. "Very well, Mama."

At that, Mrs. Bennet turned to me. I was prepared to add a ridiculous sum to the amount she had already extracted from her daughter. "What is your favorite color, Mr. Darcy?" Before I could reply, she addressed Miss Elizabeth. "That rose gown that Lydia had made will be just the thing!"

"But I—"

"Yes, the rose shall do very well. Much better than that old blue gown you insist on wearing."

"I like blue."

Miss Elizabeth's resolve had remained unwaveringly firm until the mention of the assembly. Imagining how much mending a household of five ladies would produce and how precious to her the small amount of her pin money must be, I suspected that gaining her mother's silence must have come at significant cost. The least I could do was cooperate.

"Blue is my favorite color," I interjected before Mrs. Bennet added more distasteful conditions to her daughter's gracious compromise.

Mrs. Bennet bunched her chin. "Blue? Are you certain? Most gentlemen do not know their own minds when it comes to ladies' fashion."

I straightened to my full height. "I am a gentleman of a strong mind and firm opinions."

"Please, Mama, turn so that Mr. Darcy may depart. We still need to rinse your hair."

Finally, Mrs. Bennet complied, and both ladies disappeared under the tree roots. Having little guarantee that Mrs. Bennet would remain with her back toward me, I hastened out of the water, grabbed my garments, and attempted to dress behind a prickly bush that stabbed me repeatedly when it was not snagging my linens. I was certain my poor valet would bemoan taking his leave from Vienna once he saw the state of my clothing.

If clothing myself this morning had been awkward, arraying damp skin in haste and with an only semi-trustworthy female audience nearby made it doubly so. My doeskins felt crooked, as did my shirt. The buttons did not align properly; I dared not take the time to fix them. It would be necessary to sneak up the servant's stairs from the kitchen to my bedchamber. I would have to endure Weller's disapproval, but I was desperate to avoid being seen by anyone else who would rightly demand an explanation for my disheveled state.

Miraculously, the seams of my strained breeches did not burst when I mounted my horse, or I would have suffered even further humiliation. I rode up the bank with the sound of Mrs. Bennet's chatter fading behind me.

"Oh, Lizzy! Such strong legs, and such—"

"Mama, you promised!"

"I promised to be silent to everyone else, not to you!"

I did not linger to hear her daughter's clever reply. I had to sneak inside Netherfield, make myself presentable, and return with a rope before my reckless-ness diminished the Gardiner children's diversion at the stream.

The stable boy said nothing to me when he took my horse. Mrs. Ramsay only lifted her eyebrows and pointed me to the staircase the servants used that would lead the closest to my bedchamber.

I took the stairs quietly, opening the door slowly and closing it softly as I looked down both lengths of the hall. It was clear. I quickly padded down the hall to my suite, a sigh of relief puffing my cheeks as I slipped inside my rooms... and froze.

Richard sat at my writing desk, swirling a drink in one hand.

"Sir!" exclaimed my reddening valet. His chest heaved up and down, and his jaw dropped to his chest. Weller was too polite to say more. I could not say the same for my trespassing cousin.

"What are you doing here?" I snapped at Richard.

He downed his drink. "You disappeared without a word. I was concerned. Poor Weller here was beside himself. Now stop pretending that we are in the wrong and tell me why you arrive in this"—he waved his hand at me—"appalling state."

Weller took a step back, his way of bowing out of a confrontation in which he wanted no part.

Richard twirled his glass on the table. "If you do not have an explanation worthy of your behavior, I shall be greatly put out."

What had I done to deserve this harsh punishment? I gritted my teeth and prepared for the worst.

My door burst open, and Bingley rushed inside. "Darcy! There you are! I have been looking all over for you!" He stopped in place. "Dear God, what happened to you? Why are you in this..." He waved his hand around.

Richard supplied the words. "Appalling state."

I sighed and accepted the circumstances, which

could not get any worse now unless someone else walk into my room. I reached into the bottom drawer of my desk, pulled out the good brandy, and poured three glasses. I had a fourth ready, but Weller declined. With a shrug, I tossed the contents of one down my gullet and promptly refilled the glass.

Brandy ready, audience anticipating, I said with all the dignity I could muster, "First, allow me to make myself presentable."

Chapter Ten

For the third time this week, I saw Weller's nostrils flare and his lips pinch. He did not utter one word. None were needed.

I felt Richard and Bingley watching me—laughing at me. It grated on my pride, but I refused to let it show or make Weller suffer from my deteriorating mood.

Clasping my hands in front of me penitently, I bowed my head. "I shall not make it a custom to add to your duties as I have done lately. My sincerest apologies."

Weller sighed so deeply that his shoulders rose, but his voice was proud as he spoke. "I packed more than enough shirts and doeskins to see you properly attired for the duration of your stay here, sir. I thank you for taking greater care of your boots, as the second pair I ordered from Hoby will not be ready for another month, and your second best are hardly acceptable."

They were the most comfortable pair of boots I had ever owned, the first made for me by Hoby. I was loath to part with them despite Weller's poor opinion of the worn leather and scuff marks. "I shall take extra precautions with my boots," I assured him.

He nodded approval. "Shall I order a bath drawn?"

His eyes flickered over to where Richard and Bingley still sat, listening. Weller would not hesitate to evict them from my chambers, and I was sorely tempted to set him loose upon my unwelcome guests. However, I preferred that they hear me relate the story rather than anyone else. Much as I appreciated Miss Elizabeth's attempts to silence her mother, my confidence in Mrs. Bennet's ability to hold her tongue was about as great as Weller's confidence in me at the moment.

"No bath, thank you. I must make haste to return."

Stepping behind the dressing screen, I began relating the events of the morning to Richard and Bingley while Weller assisted me into freshly pressed and brushed garments. His expression was indecipherable as I described the exchange between myself and the Bennet ladies, and I noticed he took as much care with the selection of my waistcoat and the folds of my cravat as he did before a ball or a night at the theater. It was apparent that my recent recklessness with my wardrobe had not adversely affected his exemplary standards.

He picked the wrinkled mass of clothing up from

the floor, pinching them between his fingers, and then departed from the dressing room with an audible sigh.

Richard clucked his tongue. "Such a spectacular affectation of martyrdom. If you do not take care, my brother will finally have his way and snatch Weller out from under your nose. It would serve you right."

Bingley nodded. "Good valets are difficult to find." Turning to me, he asked, "Did you really damage my neighbor's property?"

Richard shook his head. "That is not the right question, Bingley." He turned to face me, his lips twitching. "Did you really expose your white rump to two innocent ladies?"

My face flamed.

Rising to his feet, Richard clapped me on the back with his smile widening and his voice straining to contain his merriment. "Never fear, old man. The sight would surely have blinded them... or made them wish they were blind." He guffawed loudly.

My temper snapped. "At least I have a posterior. One would have to look for yours with a magnifying glass."

Bingley coughed and turned to the door. "Come, let us check the barn. I believe that is the most likely place to find a rump—er, I mean, a rope."

The three of us stood in tense silence. I would not be the first one to give in when it took all my effort to remain vexed. I did not wish to encourage their mockery. Clenching my fists and bunching my shoulders by my ears, I stalked out of my room and out to the stables.

The groom had coiled up a generous length of sturdy rope, much thicker than the flimsy line that had frayed in my hands that morning. Looping it over my shoulder, I hinted yet again that I did not require any further assistance to two pairs of determinedly deaf ears. So I spoke more directly. "I do not wish for company."

"It is not good for you to always get what you wish, Darcy. I would not miss this for the world," said Richard.

"Nobody else will be there," I argued.

"Just as nobody was supposed to be there this morning?"

I clenched my jaw. Lord, he could be annoying.

"You cannot expect me to stay behind when I am responsible for the behavior of my guests." Bingley sounded as though I were a blustering idiot for whom he must apologize.

"Excellent point, Bingley," agreed Richard. "Very honorable. I just want to see Darcy make a cake of himself again."

Once again, Bingley coughed and turned away. Richard was a bad influence on him.

I endured their jabs all the way downstream where the river narrowed enough to cross, and then to the sprawling oak tree, where, to my acute dismay, the Gardiners were already swimming.

Sitting atop the branch was Miss Elizabeth, her bare feet dangling over either side of the limb. She tugged at her bathing gown, and I pretended not to notice. Richard and Bingley were too enchanted by Miss Bennet to look up from the blanket on which she sat with her niece. Her lap was full of daisies she was twisting into jewelry for the little girl, who was already adorned with a crown and necklace of the delicate flower.

"Gentlemen! How good it is to see you again! I feared our paths would not cross again before we depart for London," called Mr. Gardiner.

Mrs. Gardiner's gaze wandered to me, then darted up to the tree where her niece was perched. Her brows furrowed. Did she wonder why I was here with a rope?

The glint in Richard's eye told me that he noticed, too. When he opened his mouth to speak, I knew I must beat him to it before he spilled the entire tale in the most mortifying manner.

Fortunately, before either of us could utter a word, Miss Elizabeth said, "You are a man of your word, Mr. Darcy. Thank you for fetching a thicker rope."

I appreciated how she glossed over my unintentional vandalism, turning my error into an honorable, thoughtful deed. While her explanation seemed to satisfy her aunt's curiosity, the arch of Richard's brow remained problematic. It taunted me, saying, *Yes, Darcy, and just* why *are the Bennets in need of another rope?*

It was best to make a clean breast of it. With a nod of appreciation to Miss Elizabeth for her attempt to spare me from humiliation, I told the Gardiners what had happened.

Of course, when I realized the children had stopped their activities to listen, their wide eyes fixed upon me in rapt attention, I had to choose between expressing how much my pride had suffered or rising above it with humor.

By the time my storytelling reached the sound of the frayed line smacking against my forehead, I saw my misadventure with enough amusement to merit such a story. I may even have embellished a few details for their enjoyment.

"What then, Mr. Darcy?" asked Jamie.

I paused long enough for them to lean forward. "When I opened my eyes, I did not see Peter at the pearly gates as I had feared, but Jemima Duck's webbed feet paddling over to see how I fared."

The boys giggled, as did their parents. Their little daughter, though, was all concern. "You were not hurt, were you, Mr. Darcy?"

What a dear girl! What was left of my pride after the telling melted at Esther's concern. "No," I answered softly. "I assure you that I am quite well." I pulled a roll out of my pocket and handed it to her, at which moment Jemima appeared.

Esther squealed when she saw the duck. "See, Jemima?! You are an excellent nurse. Mr. Darcy is quite well, and he has brought you a treat!" She tore off a sizable chunk and tossed it near her target.

Jemima was more interested in the treat bobbing near her than in my welfare. And I was more interested in replacing the rope than in tarrying in conversation while Miss Elizabeth dangled over our heads.

Bingley and Richard hovered around the blanket where the ladies sat. As they would have no difficulty conversing with the Gardiners, I felt free to pursue my objective.

Taking off my hat, I set it in a shaded corner on the blanket and turned to the base of the tree.

A new predicament presented itself in the fissured ridges of the mature oak's bark. I dared not scratch the boots I had sworn to Weller that I would care for. But neither could I remove them and my stockings in front of so many ladies... and certainly not in front of impressionable children who would look to me as an example of proper behavior.

Mumbling a mental apology to Weller, I began to climb.

Miss Elizabeth greeted me with a smile that reached her eyes. My heart tripped and my breath stuttered.

"I must admit, Mr. Darcy, that I misjudged you."

I had to know what she meant by that.

She continued, "You made the children laugh at your expense. You are not as proud as I had thought."

"I preferred to make you laugh. I knew it to be a

pleasant sound." Riding high on the success of my eloquent reply, my foot slipped and flailed clumsily about until I grabbed a sturdier branch.

Miss Elizabeth was at my side, lending me support. "You ought to have removed your boots. Propriety is impractical when climbing a tree." She looked pointedly down at her bare feet.

I ought to have been offended to see a young lady's exposed ankles and toes—for the second time—and I really ought not to have looked at them for as long as I did. But the only clear thought I could form was that it was a pity to cover such fine appendages with stockings.

She let go of my arm and stepped away, which allowed me to find my tongue. Clearing my throat, I said, "A liberty you rightly took, not suspecting that three gentlemen would intrude on the scene."

"You are not an intrusion."

A silence where every passing second added more meaning, more questions, passed between us. She took another step farther down the thick branch. "We are always pleased to receive our neighbors and their guests."

I was just a neighbor—Bingley's guest. Why should that rankle me? That was an apt description. She had no reason to be any happier to see me than she would to see Bingley or Richard.

Instead of returning to the safety of the ground now that I was here, she continued down the length of the limb close to where she had left her rope draped. "May I assist you down?" I called after her.

She spun back around to face me. "Why?"

"So I may tie this rope for you?" I had thought the reason for my offer was obvious.

She looked at my boot-clad feet. "And allow you to slip and fall?"

"I would no sooner allow you to suffer a similar accident."

"I am not the one who nearly slipped a moment ago. Perhaps *I* ought to offer to assist *you*."

How did she did not see the blatant impropriety of her continuing aloft in a bathing gown where anyone below might see... things? "It is immodest."

Miss Elizabeth lifted her chin and responded testily. "If you must know, I always wear breeches beneath it. If they are good enough for Princess Charlotte, then they are good enough for me."

Princess Charlotte had begun wearing drawers under her clothing, to the shock of the *ton*. I had not given the matter any consideration until now. Although my reaction was not entirely favorable, I had to admit that, under the present circumstances, a lady's use of breeches was practical. Still, I was a gentleman. And I had already contemplated the benefits of ladies' undergarments for an inappropriate amount of time.

I cleared my throat again. "Pray allow me to assist you so that I might fasten the rope."

"Please see reason, Mr. Darcy. I am lighter than you and have a better grip on the branch."

On this matter, I could not rightly budge. I was a gentleman. "I cannot overlook your welfare to spare mine."

She did not immediately protest, so I pressed my advantage. "If you will allow me passage, I can climb out farther." I stepped closer, not knowing how to trade places with her without us both toppling into the river or ending up in a scandalous embrace. I was pondering the most effective manner to perform such a logistic maneuver when she spun away from me and swung her legs up and onto the branch above us. She hung there, the loose fabric of her bathing gown flapping away from me. Leaning her head back, her gleeful eyes met mine. "We may avoid any potentially immodest behavior if you just walk below me and watch where you step, Mr. Darcy."

Impertinent minx!

Her loose tendrils tickled my face as I passed beneath her, and the temptation to linger nearly overwhelmed me. With a burst of disciplined resolve, I scrambled past her. Turning in her direction, I lowered myself down to sit on the limb without so much as a peek upward and dedicated my full attention to tying the new rope.

I did not look up when she sat opposite me, but I was keenly aware of her every move.

"Why are you tying the knot so loose?" She leaned forward for a closer look.

"If I tie the rope too tightly around the limb, it will become weak as the tree continues to grow around it. This looser knot is better for the tree and should last longer."

She considered for a moment, then she pointed at the bowline. "May I try?"

Unwrapping the rest of the rope draped over my shoulder, I held the other end of the rope out to her. The hemp was rough to the touch, but she did not flinch as she took it.

"Over and around? Like this?" She tugged it tight before I could correct her. It snarled and tangled.

"Close, but not quite. Here, allow me to show you." Our hands brushed in the exchange. I wished my palms were not so sweaty. Wiping them against my breeches, I explained each twist and turn before pulling the bowline knot tight.

"And it unties so easily!" she exclaimed, plucking the rope from my hands to attempt the knot herself. "It is loose when no weight is on it, but when it is being used, it tightens itself. It is brilliant!" She held up her knot for me to admire.

I could not help but admire her skill. "You swim well, and you climb trees expertly, and now you tie ropes—"

She laughed. "Yes, Mr. Darcy, I am a proper hoyden."

I had always thought it was a gentleman's duty to spare the ladies in his company from every discomfort, and I still believed it was important to see to a lady's well-being. Until today, I had not met a lady who actually wished to learn and take part in those same duties. While I gladly would have spared Miss Elizabeth the scratches on her hands from the rough line and the soreness she was likely to feel on the morrow from lifting and holding the heavy length of rope, I could not do so without depriving her of an experience she clearly desired.

What a singular woman! She did not complain or tire. Also absent were the supercilious compliments most ladies made about my strength, although I would not have minded hearing them from her.

"How did you learn to tie knots like this?" she asked.

"My uncle." My father's youngest brother had been a brave man, eager for adventure and always in the thick of activity. I missed his vivacity, his stories. I missed *him.* "He sailed with Admiral Nelson to Aboukir Bay."

"The Battle of the Nile? I secretly hoped they would discover the library of Alexandria while they were there. I mourn the loss of so many books."

"You do not think the library is a myth? There is no evidence to prove it ever existed." It had simply vanished. While I wished to believe in it, my skeptical nature was not satisfied.

"I was convinced enough to attempt to learn Greek."

"And were your efforts successful?"

"Ípe o gáidaros ton petíno kefála," she rattled off.

A barkish laugh escaped me. "The donkey called the rooster big-headed?"

"It only sounds intelligent when my audience does not understand its meaning." She shrugged. "It is all I remember from my studies."

"It is a memorable phrase."

"Yes, it does roll off the tongue, does it not?"

"And it sounds much more polite than 'that is the pot calling the kettle black.'"

"Only because most people do not know Greek."

"Their loss is our convenience."

She brightened. "I shall have to find an occasion to use it now. Only, I doubt anyone of my acquaintance would understand my little joke."

"I would." I knew I was flirting. Even so, I said the words.

"Yes. Well, considering how unflattering such a mutually applicable comment would be to both of us, let us hope I never have occasion to utter it."

Richard called loudly, "Are you two finished hanging that rope, or do you intend to sit up there all day? The brave Masters Gardiner must have another opportunity to swing before they depart."

I resented the interruption, but I rose to my feet. As impractical as it was, I offered Miss Elizabeth my arm, as though the few feet to the tree's trunk were as simple as a stroll down a paved path.

She glanced at my proffered arm, her brow arching. "Do you mean to make both of us fall? Perhaps I should offer you *my* arm."

Me, take a lady's arm? Heaven forfend!

Shifting my weight to prove the superiority of my steadiness, my boot slipped at the same moment she gently nudged my arm away.

Chapter Eleven

I should have taken off my boots.

Richard leaned closer to Mr. Gardiner. "An expedient way of getting down... but too soggy for my taste."

Mr. Gardiner's shoulders shook. Unlike Richard, he did not laugh aloud, and I appreciated the man's self-control.

By the time I waded to the bank and onto the grass, Miss Elizabeth had climbed down the tree. I caught a momentary glimpse of concern in her eyes before the line between her brows smoothed. Her lips relaxed except for one tempting corner that curled upward. "I did not think I pushed you so hard, sir. My apologies."

I could not allow her to assume the blame for my unsteadiness. "I ought to have removed my boots."

Miss Elizabeth bit her bottom lip as her smile spread. She would say something impertinent and clever, and I rather looked forward to it. I leaned closer, waiting, impervious to Richard's laughter. He had no restraint.

"Oh, no, Mr. Darcy, I cannot allow you to absolve me of guilt by assuming all the fault."

The twinkle in her eye dared me to tease in turn. "It *is* my fault. Had I removed my boots, I would not have lost my balance so easily."

"Oh, yes, Mr. Darcy, it is entirely your fault. Had you not insisted on helping me replace the rope, your boots would not be ruined. Only a gentleman would have insisted as you did."

How was I supposed to reply to that? To disagree would be to my discredit, but to agree would sound proud. Her reasoning rendered me mute and charmed.

This is a woman who would tie society into tongue-tied knots in minutes. I would love to be in my aunt's drawing room when she met Elizabeth Bennet.

"It is all your fault, and I shall not deny you the honor of assuming the blame which is rightfully yours." She quirked her eyebrow and curtsied, to which I bowed as though she had bestowed upon me a highly coveted accolade.

I stopped myself before I thanked her, for that really would be too much.

Mr. Gardiner handed me my coat, and I draped it over my arm, knowing full well that no amount of contortions would help me into it. But it could cover the doeskin clinging scandalously to my thighs. I really should depart.

I had just bowed to take my leave when Esther came and stood directly before me with my hat in her little hands. "I made your hat pretty," she said.

Thank goodness my first reaction was to gasp rather than groan. She had strung a loop of daisies together around the brim, a cheerful crown to adorn my beaver hat.

I took the proffered item. She clasped her hands behind and swayed from side to side, cheeks pink, eyes gleaming. I was fully aware I would be teased mercilessly if I wore it. However, the child had worked so hard, I could show nothing but pleasure at being the recipient of her generosity.

Tilting the hat to better admire her handiwork from all angles, I nodded in approval and placed the flower-bedecked hat on my head at an angle.

"Very pretty," agreed Richard.

I refrained from drawing his cork.

Bingley added, "I rather wish I had a crown of daisies for my hat."

Esther beamed. Despite my companions' mockery, my chest puffed with pride. I would have leaned closer to Esther's height, but I feared testing the strength of the seams of my trousers, so I merely lowered my voice. "It is the most thoughtful gift anyone has given me in many years."

She leaped at me, wrapping her skinny arms around my middle.

Her mother and father lunged forward toward her, both exclaiming in unison, "Esther!"

I waved them off, for the girl's reaction had been borne of sincerity—it would be wrong to chastise her for it. I only wished I was not so wet.

With one last squeeze, she let go and stepped away, looking bashful now that the consequence of her impulsive display was upon her.

I would have none of it. "It is my sincerest hope that you and your family will allow me to welcome you as guests at Pemberley. I have a sister who would love to meet you, a rope swing at a pond which has been sorely neglected these many years, and a Cook with a penchant for making too many strawberry tarts."

Her brothers eagerly offered their services, declaring their appetites superior to their little sister.

"That is very generous of you, Mr. Darcy," said Mr. Gardiner. "We had hoped to travel north this summer with our niece."

Which niece? Miss Elizabeth's contented smile answered my question.

"The larger your party, the merrier we shall be," I replied, ignoring Richard and Bingley's exchange of glances. True, I was not inclined to enjoy large parties, but their reaction was exaggerated.

Jemima shook her tail and quacked by my feet. Instinctively, I patted my pocket, but it was empty.

Esther giggled. "Can Jemima come too?"

"Of course," I said. For just a moment, I forgot I was sopping wet. But a shift in my weight made my boots squish and squeak, reminding me that I really must depart while I had a shred of modesty remaining.

Carefully, I bowed and bid them a good day. The boys lost no time testing out the new rope, and I used their distraction to mount my horse, which, to my great relief, I was able to accomplish without further incident.

With a farewell tip of my flowered hat, I departed with Richard and Bingley.

"Pretty hats and large parties... I am all anticipation for the next time you see Miss Elizabeth, for you say the most astounding things in her presence."

I could not deny it, so I did not try.

With no reaction to fuel Richard's badgering, the teasing soon stopped. He and Bingley were content to praise the Gardiners and Bennets. By the time we reached Netherfield, we were a merry trio.

It was not until they entered the house ahead of me to clear my path from unwanted observers that my humor settled. I had broken a promise and must face the consequences.

Taking a deep breath, I opened the door to my bedchamber and waited.

Weller did not tarry to join me. At the sight before him, his step halted. "Sir!"

I bowed my head. "Weller, you have served me

well. If you wish to give your notice, I will provide you with the highest recommendation and praise, though it would sadden me deeply to see you go."

He bunched his cheeks. "Did the young lady see you before… this?"

Now I understood why he had taken such pains with my waistcoat and cravat. Nothing remained of his meticulous attentions, and I did not even have a compliment to pass on to him. Not that Miss Elizabeth was the sort of young lady to flatter a man's vanity. She certainly had not flattered mine. More often than not, she laughed at me. And now that I could appreciate the ridiculousness of the circumstances of our few meetings, I found myself inclined to laugh as well. At least she had seen me presentable before I splashed into the stream. "She did," I assured him.

His gaze fixed on my ruined boots, and my contrition swiftly returned. "I am sorry. I made a promise, and I broke it."

Weller sniffed and tugged at the bottom of his waistcoat. "It will take both of us to remove those boots." Was that a hint of a smile?

He did not ask for the cause of this carnage, which was perhaps why I felt more inclined to tell him how I ended up, fully clothed, in the stream.

Once suited in an ensemble of clean, dry garments, I stood before the mirror while Weller brushed the shoulders of my dinner coat.

"Even a dutiful man is entitled to act his age on

occasion." That said, he turned to my hat and gingerly plucked the daisy crown off the brim. Sadly, they were already wilting. I should have removed them before now, but I didn't have the heart to. I could not bear to see them thrown into the hearth, which was what would be done soon enough. "We may not be able to preserve the crown as it is, but a few of these blooms will dry nicely."

His idea was perfect. "Thank you, Weller."

Daisies draped carefully over his hands, he opened the door just as Richard appeared, dressed in riding coat and boots.

"I did not wish to leave without saying goodbye."

"You are leaving now?"

Richard nodded curtly. "I have little desire to ride in the rain, which would be my lot should I delay my departure. I trust you intend to stay on?" he asked with a sly grin.

I had intended to leave with Richard two days hence, but I could not leave now. Besides, I had told Sir William that I would attend his assembly. It would be rude to go back on my word and break yet another promise. One was bad enough.

"I thought not." Richard clapped me on the back. "I wish you every happiness."

"Do not congratulate me as though I were the groom at a wedding. I hardly know her."

Again, that devilish twinkle. "Are you considering marriage, Darcy?"

Oh, how I wished I could rephrase that.

"Interesting," he said with a smirk.

I clamped my mouth shut. He did have a point. How quickly my thoughts had turned to matrimony! Miss Elizabeth was dangerous. By all rights, I ought to avoid her like the plague.

But I counted the hours, the minutes, until I might see her again.

Chapter Twelve

After ten days of heat and hazy skies, the empty cold and harsh rain cast a gloomy shroud over Netherfield Park. Even Bingley succumbed to melancholy the following morning when it became apparent that we could not go to the stream.

I, too, missed the exercise. Richard was gone. I told myself that those were the reasons for my dejection, but it was a lie. I missed her—a young lady I had only just met, but to whom I was tied by some invisible string. Elizabeth was my Rome—every thought led me to her.

I had always prided myself on my certainty, my ability to determine the right way to proceed in any situation, and then to act. But Elizabeth was such a mixture of right and wrong, of black and white contrasts. The wisest course would be to avoid her entirely. And yet, I could not. Nor did I want to. Not at all.

Bingley's sisters were happier. They seemed to suffer the delusion that I enjoyed their company without realizing that I avoided them as much as possible. I would spend the day between the library and the billiard room, where I currently was, as these rooms were least likely to be inhabited by either of them.

Why did I resist avoiding Elizabeth when it was so easy to avoid Miss Bingley?

I leaned over the table and aimed my cue. The ivory balls scattered and clacked, reminding me of the crack of the tree branch and a certain pair of fine eyes dancing with mirth.

Straightening my posture, I raked my hand through my hair, trying to rid myself of the image. It took a few minutes, but I eventually succeeded... until a shimmer of polished wood reminded me of the shimmer in her hair. The blue velvet sashes holding back the curtains were a similar shade to her bathing gown. The bourbon in my glass glowed like the golden flecks in her eyes.

I slammed the cue onto the table. This had to stop. I am not, nor have I ever been, a creature led by emotions, and I was not about to concede to them now. I was a Darcy, for Heaven's sake!

Downing the rest of my drink, I paced the room, enumerating each rational argument with every stride. There was her indolent father. Yes, Mr. Bennet possessed a quick wit and a sense of humor I could appreciate. However, from what I had seen, he managed his daughters' welfare and encouraged their prospects as well as he presided over his estate—poorly. Should I reward such negligent behavior by showing an interest in one of his daughters? He would be delighted to saddle me with the responsibility of supporting all five! And the man would learn nothing other than to continue indulging his laxity until he had ruined his family and his estate. It was a story with no happy ending.

And yet... could I stand by and allow it to happen? Would I deny Elizabeth a chance to improve her lot and that of her sisters merely to spite a man too lazy to improve his behavior? Should she continue to suffer from her father's poor decisions? Ought she not to have a choice in the matter?

These questions sounded presumptuous, even in my own mind. I was making myself out to be her savior! As if she needed my help. I hardly knew her!

But was that true? I knew that she climbed trees expertly, flipped nimbly from rope swings, swam like a fish, persuaded her determined mother to preserve both her freedom and mine, and had a face that lit up like a candle when her uncle spoke of their upcoming trip to the north this summer. Elizabeth cherished her independence, and she did not shy away from adventure. A lady like this would wish to have more choices.

Would she choose me? A shiver shook through me

and twisted my stomach. What if she did not choose me? Did I want her to?

Why do I care?

Gritting my teeth, I resumed pacing and engaged my reason once again. Mrs. Bennet. One brief encounter was sufficient for me to develop a headache. Imagining her as my guest at Pemberley worsened the pounding in my skull. She would make herself a frequent guest. Keeping her conversation under good regulation would be a challenge; she would not be welcome in certain circles—my own family, for one.

But she had kept her promise and held her tongue. Otherwise, word of "the incident" would have spread. Not one maid or footman had considered me with a knowing glance or greeted me with strained expressions or suppressed laughter. Weller would have alerted me to any pertinent household gossip. Mrs. Bennet could be trusted to keep her word—an admirable trait. Perhaps it was possible to persuade her to improve her behavior since her daughters stood to benefit.

I caught myself before I built a convincing case in Mrs. Bennet's defense. This could not be borne!

My life had always been guided by facts and logic. Any gentleman would have to consider the harsh reality which would certainly result from attaching himself to a family such as the Bennets. I had expectations to live up to, reputations to maintain, duties to perform. I would be a fool to form such an attachment.

You are a fool.

Squeezing my hands into fists, I turned to the window. Dark clouds stretched out as far as I could see. Rain battered against the sun-hardened ground, much like my relentless thoughts. Did I provoke even a fraction of the feeling in Elizabeth that she provoked in me? Did she think of me as I thought of her?

I leaned against the billiard table. Arguing against her merits felt like a personal assault. I knew, clear to the marrow of my bones, that where it most mattered—values, beliefs, ideals, intellect, interests—Elizabeth was my match. She was not after my purse, or my standing, or anything else by which she might gain profit at my expense. There had been many opportunities for her to take advantage of my honor, but she had not.

I did not trust easily, but I trusted Elizabeth. I would be a fool to pursue her; I would be a worse fool not to.

One smile from her would knock me off my feet, as she had done literally every time since our first meeting. Next time, instead of landing on my backside, I might end up on one knee. It was not a decision to be made casually—and all for an impertinent miss who was more likely than most to refuse me.

Lightning cracked through the darkness, illuminating the room. Thunder rolled over the heavens. I pulled a chair closer to the window, searching for solace in the tumult.

Chapter Thirteen

F ive days later, the storm had calmed, but the rain poured relentlessly. Ponds near the house swelled; water collected in pools spotted around the drive—ripe for splashing. When I was a boy, I would have stomped with both feet to see how far the water would splatter. That was before I realized how much extra work I was causing the maid tasked with the wash.

"More coffee, Mr. Darcy?" Miss Bingley asked, her hand on the urn.

I nodded. How would Miss Bingley rationalize my conduct if I marched out of doors this minute to splash in the puddles?

"You look pleased." She poured and purred. "It is no wonder when we may enjoy each other's conversation in greater intimacy."

A gentleman could not continue to smile under

such a threat. "I was admiring the exceptional drainage of Bingley's property."

Her eye twitched. "Drainage?"

Maintaining a stoic mien, I kept my tone level. "It is a subject which occupies the time and attention of every gentleman of property, and it pleases me greatly to see evidence that Bingley has chosen a well-drained estate."

Bingley sat taller. "Of course, it remains to be seen how the fields and the tenants' houses fare."

"True, but has not your bailiff assured you that not one roof has leaked?"

"There was one, but the farmer who lived there was able to patch it until it is safer to fix."

"And the lower flooded fields are not causing any damage to your property or your neighbors."

"Not that I am aware of, and Landon knows to inform me immediately if that changes."

"Your consideration is certain to win your servants' respect and your neighbors' admiration."

My friend's chest swelled, and he seemed to grow another inch in his chair.

"I am shocked they have not canceled the assembly." After so many soft compliments, Mrs. Hurst's sharp voice offended my ears.

Bingley's brows met. "Why should you suggest that? The bridges are in fine order. The roads are wet, but they are not impassable. There is no sound reason for the assembly to be canceled."

Miss Bingley rolled her eyes. "I should think it obvious, Charles. Only look through the windowpane."

He did, and he appeared no more enlightened than he had been before. Nor was I.

She rolled her eyes with a sigh. "It is dangerous. We cannot be expected to travel in this rain. If they had any consideration for our safety and the delicate silk of our gowns, they would cancel."

She would spoil everyone's fun to spare a couple of gowns? I tried to sound patient, but I did not feel it. "It is the village's monthly assembly. Surely you would not wish to deny the tenants, shopkeepers, and their families the opportunity to eat, drink, and dance."

"They are not in our circle and therefore may do whatever they please. I only wish they would not insist on involving us in their affairs," she replied sourly.

Our circles? Had she become so elevated in her own mind that she considered herself above all the local residents? She clearly did not understand the role of a landowner. "Your brother is wise to seize the opportunity to make himself known to the very people you would slight." She squirmed in her chair, and I continued, "As the newest occupants of this estate, Bingley must establish himself. His tenants' welfare depends on his ability to oversee his land and their dwellings capably. Allowing himself to be approached in an informal setting will go a long way in gaining their trust and encouraging conversation."

"We must establish ourselves, Caroline. The

assembly is the perfect opportunity for us to do that. Rain or not, I intend to go."

Miss Bingley said nothing. She had sensed my disapproval and would not argue against me, but her pinched expression displayed her displeasure.

I crossed my arms and narrowed my eyes at her, letting her feel the full effect of my best glower.

Bingley's face reddened. "Is not any endeavor one wants to achieve worth a little discomfort?"

Miss Bingley snapped. "Oh, Charles, you assume we want to go. Where would the benefit be? I do not understand why you do not listen to me when you know me to be right!"

Mrs. Hurst nodded. "The locals will benefit from our influence, but I doubt we shall enjoy any benefit from the association."

Her brother sputtered, "As the newest family to settle in the area, it befits us to attend. We must meet our neighbors. Already we have met families of quality, and—"

"Here?" she interrupted. "Who? We have only met Sir William and that indiscreet family at the stream. They would be the laughingstock of the *ton* with their assumed airs and haughty impertinence."

"No, Miss Bingley, that would be you." I tightened my fingers into a fist and stood from the breakfast table. Hot indignation pounded through me, and yet the cold calm in my voice would have made my mother proud. "You condemn them when you do not know them, raise yourself above their company when you could benefit from their instruction far more than they could possibly benefit from yours."

Miss Bingley tittered uneasily. "Only if I wish to learn more about St. James." She looked about the table for support.

She did not think I was serious, and it became imperative for me to make her understand how serious I was. "I stand with Bingley. Rain or not, I intend to go to the assembly this evening where I intend to dance with every Bennet and Lucas lady in attendance. Now, if you will excuse me, I must make preparations."

I left the room to silence. It was too early to dress for the assembly, but I had a point to make. Without pausing, I continued up the stairs to my bedchamber.

Weller sat by the window, holding my scuffed boot up to the dim light to inspect with a polish rag in his other hand. He rose when he saw me and gestured to the bed, where several waistcoats lay like a colorful coverlet. "I did not know which color you would prefer, so I pressed several. You do not happen to know what color your young lady will be wearing?"

My young lady? I opened my mouth to correct him, but my defensive reply would only encourage his disbelief. Closing my mouth, I shook my head, and then I remembered. "Her favorite color is blue."

"Very well, sir. The blue it is." He held up my old boots. "These will do to get you so far as the assembly, where you will change into your slippers."

I had been so intent on proving my point to Miss Bingley and Mrs. Hurst, it was not until this moment that the full implication of my decision crashed over me. I would see Elizabeth again. I would not be able to avoid her. Thanks to my impulsive tirade, I would most certainly ask her to dance with me.

Not that dancing with Elizabeth would be a trial. Only that we would talk and she would be charming and I would fall harder.

A knock sounded at the door. Bingley stood in the aperture, shoulders by his ears, hands fisted at his side, like a coil about to spring.

"Come in." I gestured to a chair.

He walked by the chair, then turned to pace the other way, his fists clasped behind his back. "I remember a conversation I had with the colonel about risk and regret. He advised me that one cannot live without taking some risks, that the ones worth taking are the risks which I would most regret not taking. Even if I fail, that I should not dwell on the mistake but on what I can learn from it."

That sounded like something Richard would say. Sound counsel, if not a bit... risky.

Bingley turned to face me, his fingers gripping the back and squeaking against the wood of the chair he would not sit on. "It was sound advice—advice I have attempted to practice to guide my choices. I was terrified to take this property and all the responsibility that came with it, but I know that I would have regretted not taking the chance to prove myself, to become the master not only of a fine estate but of my own life."

Risk. Regret. I had spent most of my life avoiding the first and, while I had not avoided the latter, I could live with the regrets I had.

Courting Elizabeth was a tremendous risk—the greatest of my life. But could I live with the regret of losing her completely?

The mere thought kicked me in the gut, sucked the air out of my lungs, and gripped my heart. Losing her would be my deepest regret. And I did not know if I could bear it.

Bingley groaned and fell into the chair, his head in his hands. Not the reaction one expected from a gentleman successfully proving himself to be more capable than he had believed himself.

"What is wrong?" I asked.

He spoke from behind his hands. "I do not suppose that your coachman has returned from visiting his sister?"

"No. He does not return until next week."

Dropping his hands, he sat up, a sigh of resignation seeping from his pursed lips. "My coachman has fallen ill. He cannot drive us into Meryton." He scrunched his face. "And if that is not bad enough, I had to add my two cents to my sisters after you quit the room. I meant to take advantage of your firmness to establish my own."

"Well done."

"Thank you, but now both of us shall have to eat humble pie. Any ground I might have gained with them will certainly be flung in my face for months."

For myself, I could not have cared less. But Bingley was another matter. "Is your coachman being seen to?"

"The apothecary is on his way... a Mr. Jones from Meryton."

"Very good. Have you talked to your housekeeper? She will know what is in the still room."

"Yes, and yes. Mrs. Nicholls already sent ginger tea."

"Well done. Now, is there no replacement? A capable footman or an apprentice? The distance is not far, and the roads are passable, but I suspect there will be many ruts and holes to maneuver around."

Bingley rubbed his hands against his trousers until a thought struck him. His face lit up as brightly as his hair, and he clapped his hands together. "I have got it! It is a risk, but it will get us to the assembly and back."

A risk. If my inclination was to be trusted, it would be the first of several I would take that evening.

Chapter Fourteen

"If you had listened to me, Charles, we would not be in this predicament." Miss Bingley rubbed her right knee where her brother's walking stick had smacked against her and blew the feather from her sister's hat away from her face on her left side.

Bingley wedged his walking stick between himself and the carriage door. "If I listened to you, we would not be on our way to the ball at all!"

Mrs. Hurst hissed at her brother. "If you hit Caro with that walking stick one more time, I shall have Hurst throw it out of the window."

Hurst, who sat beside me opposite the disgruntled siblings, glowered at Bingley, no doubt resenting being put upon to do anything at all.

Another jolt lurched the conveyance and sent Bingley's walking stick flying at Hurst's face. He knocked it away just in time. Unfortunately, it landed on Miss Bingley's lap once again, earning Bingley another scorching look.

"I am terribly sorry!" he said yet again, fumbling with the walking stick until Hurst grabbed it away from him. He could not throw it out of the window without causing further bodily injury, or that might have been the last Bingley ever saw of his latest nod to gentlemanly fashion.

I hated to agree with Mrs. Hurst about anything, but Bingley was a danger with the thing.

The carriage jostled again.

Miss Bingley's nostrils flared. "Do we have to hit every hole between Netherfield and Meryton?"

Mrs. Hurst narrowed her eyes in the coachman's direction. "You will have to dismiss him as soon as we return to Netherfield."

"Really, Charles, a stable hand driving a coach?" Miss Bingley smoothed her skirts, her gaze flickering to me before settling on her brother. "Had you listened to me, we would be quite comfortable in the drawing room."

"And miss the assembly? I would not dream of it, Caro! And I will not dismiss James. His father was our father's coachman. He is capable and only requires some practice."

"But must you permit him to practice on us?"

"If it gets us to the ball, yes!" Bingley exclaimed, on the brink of losing his temper.

The slightest tilt of the carriage would snap the taut nerves inside, and I could not allow Bingley to bear the brunt of his sisters' animosity when my determination to get to the assembly equaled his.

Motioning for Hurst to tap the roof with Bingley's walking stick, I called, "Stop the carriage!"

Bingley shot a pointed look at Miss Bingley. "See? It is practical. Every gentleman I know has one."

"See, Charles? Mr. Darcy would prefer to walk back to Netherfield rather than endure another moment of this dreadful trip. I am covered in bruises from top to bottom."

I opened the door, carefully stepping out onto the muddy road. The chilled air pierced through my coat. Pulling the collar higher against my neck, I disabused Miss Bingley of her misunderstanding. "You will be more comfortable without me crowding you."

Bingley dashed to the other side of the carriage, plopping down beside Hurst and taking possession of his walking stick with an air of triumph.

Miss Bingley found her tongue. "Y-you do not mean to return to Netherfield?"

"In this rain? Hardly. We are closer to Meryton than to Netherfield. If I take the ribbons, perhaps your ride will not be so unsettling." I said this, not because of any exceptional skill driving a coach and four, but because I knew she would never argue against me or call my driving skills into question.

I nodded at the footman to close the door. There

was no sense in any of us getting wetter than we already were. The sooner we arrived at the stables, where there was certain to be a fire where we could dry ourselves, the better.

Climbing up to the box, I accepted the coat the lad handed to me.

He explained, "I didn't know if my coat'd have time to dry 'fore the return trip, so I asked the coachman to lend me his. If it's not offensive to you, sir, it's yours to wear."

I was already working on the buttons. "That was very thoughtful, and I thank you for it." If only Miss Bingley could see me wearing the coachman's coat—a Darcy in livery! But I was relieved to have it. The thick coat covered me from neck to boots, the wool heavy and dry. "It is a practical garment," I admired.

Eyes downcast, head bowed in defeat, the lad handed me the reins.

I did not take them. "What is your name, lad?"

"Bilby."

"I have no more knowledge of the roads than you do, Bilby. I doubt I would fare any better than you have done. But Bingley's sisters dare not complain about me, and the only way your master will arrive at Meryton in one piece is if they believe me to be holding the ribbons. Now, if you please, carry on."

Bilby's shoulders straightened. He snapped the reins and called out to the horses confidently.

Travel was slow, but we arrived at the assembly

room safely. My hair was drenched, and all the water running down my face made my shirt damp and clingy. I was loath to remove the coachman's coat.

The footman held an umbrella over the ladies while Bingley and Hurst handed them out.

I handed Bilby a few coins. "Ask for a private room where you can get dry and enjoy your repast until Bingley sends for the carriage."

"Thank you, sir, but Mr. Bingley already gave me enough. I could not rightfully accept."

"Then allow me to reward your honesty. Keep the coin. Only take care not to spend it all on ale."

Bilby chuckled. He motioned to the canopy draped over the outdoor entrance to the assembly room. "Careful not to stand under that, sir. It looks about to burst."

I climbed down. Miss Bingley greeted me with a smile. The poor footman trying to hold the umbrella over her was doing his best to shield her from the elements without slipping in the mud or disturbing the bulging canopy.

"We waited for you, Mr. Darcy. You are such a skilled driver! I hardly felt any bumps once you took the reins."

Bingley used his walking stick to point toward the entrance. "Caro, let us go inside."

She smacked his stick away. "Get that wretched weapon of injury away from me, Charles."

"You are being unreasonable."

While Miss Bingley had some protection from the elements, Bingley did not, and I needed to return the caped coat to Bilby for his use on our return.

"It is abominably wet here," she complained.

"It is perfect for the ducks," Bingley countered cheerfully.

Leaning closer to Bingley and tugging him toward the dryness under the canopy, I commented, "It is raining so hard, I half expect to see Jemima rushing down a stream into the village."

Miss Bingley batted her eyelashes at me. "What did you say, Mr. Darcy?"

Bingley replied loudly. "The duck is rushing into the village."

"Duck! Where?!" Miss Bingley shrieked, jumping to the side and slipping in the mire.

The footman tried to keep up with her, but she had spun away at an angle to smack against Bingley's side. He flailed his arms, waving his walking stick in the air.

It is a truth universally acknowledged that a gentleman in possession of a walking stick is certain to poke something with it. My instincts told me it would be the canopy. I had only time enough to steady the footman to help him avoid landing in the puddle of odorous "mud" before the inevitable happened.

The walking stick jabbed straight through the fabric, sending a concentrated cascade of water streaming through the perforation to pour directly over Miss Bingley.

Her squeal pierced my ears until she sputtered thanks to water entering her mouth.

Without a word, Bingley handed me his walking stick and ran to her side, alternately laughing and apologizing as a crowd gathered to view the spectacle.

I clamped my hand over my mouth and nudged the footman toward the carriage before her ire could settle on him. Bilby hid behind his hands, his shoulders shaking. The footman did not need my help ascending to the box, but I required the time to gain control of my composure. Just when I would think I had gained mastery over myself, I would hear Miss Bingley splutter, and I would be back where I had started.

The carriage pulled away, and I no longer had any excuse to keep me from my party.

Poor Bingley attempted to take his sister's arm, but she wanted nothing to do with him.

The two eldest Bennet sisters pushed through the crowd to Miss Bingley's side. Taking her by the shoulders, Miss Bennet gently guided Miss Bingley indoors. "Come, let us get you to the fire where you may dry. You may wear my shawl..."

Bingley followed them like a puppy does its beloved master.

Elizabeth cast a scorching look at her neighbors until they dispersed. She was a fearsome creature to behold. I felt guilty for so nearly succumbing to laughter... until her eyes locked with mine. Her lips twitched, but she contained her laughter until all the spectators had returned indoors.

I joined Elizabeth under the remnants of the canopy, wiping water and tears from my eyes in order to view her more clearly. It was the first time I had seen her wearing something other than her bathing gown. The sight of her simply took my breath away.

Chapter Fifteen

W e might have been standing in a flowered gazebo on a beautiful spring day—I hardly cared. All I saw was Elizabeth, exquisite in a blue gown that glimmered in the soft glow of the candlelight. Her bold glance met mine, and she beamed widely, the corners of her eyes crinkling.

I was captivated.

A haughty voice intruded. "Miss Elizabeth, allow me to see you inside. It is not safe to mingle with the servants." Sir William's son was not tall enough to look down his nose at me, but that did not prevent the over-dressed popinjay from trying.

The devilish twist curling Elizabeth's lips stopped me from uttering a cutting remark. Looking at me askance while addressing the young fop, she said, "This servant appears harmless to me. No more threatening to me than you are, John Lucas."

He considered me closer, his countenance conveying disbelief. He did not recognize me.

It occurred to me that I ought to be offended. Instead I was inclined to laugh. Elizabeth's influence was the cause, I was certain. Why should the young man not confuse me with a humble coachman when I still wore the servant's coat? In addition, with my hat pushed low over my forehead, Mr. Lucas could not see my face.

Playing along with Elizabeth's claim that I was harmless, I crossed my arms over my chest, puffed myself up to my fullest height, and kept my chin down, my face away from the light.

Mr. Lucas stiffened and sniffed, eyeing me narrowly. "He appears dangerous to me." He offered his arm to Elizabeth. Had he succeeded in taking her away from me, I would have been sorely tempted to prove him right.

Elizabeth stepped away from him, closer to me. She looked up, her tone serious, her eyes dancing. "Are you dangerous, sir?"

Only if that Lucas coxcomb takes you away. I could not rightly say that aloud, so I held my peace and grunted instead. That was what dangerous men did, was it not?

Patting my sleeve, her touch tingling against my arm, Elizabeth said teasingly, "Best not answer that question, Mr. Darcy."

Mr. Lucas stepped back. "Mr. Darcy? Mr. Darcy of Pemberley?"

As if there were another. I removed my hat and swept a roguish bow.

"I apologize, sir. I did not recognize you." So repentant was Mr. Lucas, so embarrassed over his blunder, I took pity on him. To his credit, his arm was no longer extended to Elizabeth. His hands were now in a prayerful position under his chin as he bowed and backed away from me.

I addressed him before he attempted to prostrate himself on the muddy ground. "No harm is done. Come, let us join the assembly."

Shedding my coat and removing my hat, I changed my gloves. I would have changed into dancing slippers had they not still been inside Bingley's carriage. *My apologies, Weller*.

Sir William swooped in like a waft of blustery air. "Mr. Darcy! I am prodigiously pleased you could make it! And I see that you have already found my eldest son. I am confident you two will become fast friends. John has had occasion to frequent St. James with me when we are in town."

Mr. Lucas did not share his father's certainty. He pulled out a handkerchief and dabbed his forehead, his eyes darting to a far corner, where he no doubt wished to disappear.

I could have allowed his discomfort to continue, but I could do nothing to dash Elizabeth's high humor.

After all, it *was* humorous. I imagined telling Richard how I sat in the rain atop the coachman's box and got confused for a servant, and I could not help but smile. Richard would never believe it.

I inclined my head to Mr. Lucas. "My house is near St. James. Perhaps you and Sir William will agree to call when you next travel to London."

Both gentlemen accepted my invitation with more enthusiasm than I was prepared to receive. By happy chance, Bingley appeared, and I motioned for him to join us.

Unfortunately, Mrs. Bennet saw my gesture and assumed it was directed toward her. Grabbing the rest of her daughters, she shoved them through the entrance hall to stand panting and preening in front of me.

On her heels was another lady whom Sir William presented as his wife, Lady Lucas, along with two daughters and another much younger son. Miss Bennet, too, emerged from a side room, where I supposed she had left Miss Bingley steaming.

Bingley always performed to advantage in such situations, so I allowed him to engage our acquaintances with friendly chatter while I leaned closer to Elizabeth.

I uttered the first thing that occurred to me. "Blue suits you."

She turned to me, regarding me with one eyebrow arched. I did not regret the compliment. I had come to the assembly prepared to flirt with Elizabeth, and I would not change course now.

With a nod, she said, "I might return the compliment."

Her gaze flicked to Mrs. Bennet, and she fingered the lace at her sleeve. "My escape from the pink gown was narrow, and you have my gratitude in securing it. However, Mama's condition was that I add more lace to this one."

"Another condition?"

She grimaced. "Yes, and they continue to accumulate. Until something happens to distract her from the advantage she holds, they will continue."

Mrs. Bennet's voice caught my attention. "What a fine figure Mr. Darcy cuts." She and Lady Lucas stood facing me. Mrs. Bennet fanned her flushed face. "And I know for a fact that he does not wear a corset or need pads to fill out his shoulders. And his seat—"

"Mama!" Elizabeth interrupted. "We can hear you!"

Everyone in the entrance hall could hear her.

Lower, and with a look that would freeze the heart of the bravest man, Elizabeth said, "You promised."

Mrs. Bennet tittered behind her fan. "Not a word from me. Not a word." Her gaze wandered down, and my face burned when I realized she was admiring my posterior. The appreciative wink she gave me confirmed she had, in fact, seen a great deal of me that day at the stream and could speak of my "seat" with some authority.

I could have died. I wished the floor would open up and swallow me whole.

She tapped my arm with her fan. "You will put in a good word for my Jane, Mr. Darcy, I hope? Mr. Bingley seems to be rather taken with her."

Bingley attended to Sir William's conversation, but his eyes lingered on Miss Bennet. He asked her to dance, and the two walked away arm in arm.

"Such a handsome couple!" Mrs. Bennet observed.

Indeed, they *were* a handsome couple, though it grated on my sensibilities to hear the mother of the lady say so aloud. Mrs. Bennet would take some getting used to.

Sensing that I could use this to gain the upper hand, I set my objections aside to negotiate with the matron. "I will put in a good word—a good word, and nothing more—on one condition." I waited until I had her full attention. It did not take long.

"Anything for my Jane!"

"You will uphold your promise to Miss Elizabeth, and you will ask no more favors from her. Her debt is paid in full."

If Mrs. Bennet was eager to accept my offer, she did not show it. She made me wait a long moment before agreeing, which is precisely what I would have done. Clearly, she was an expert negotiator. She got what she wanted.

When I caught Elizabeth's gaze and saw her admiration, I realized that I had gotten what I wanted, too. And now, I would ask her to dance.

"What a charming amusement for young people this is, Mr. Darcy!" Sir William's comment directed everyone's attention to me. "There is nothing like dancing, after all." I cringed, fearing Elizabeth would think that my request for a dance was prompted by Sir William rather than my own desire.

The gentleman yammered on. "I consider it as one of the first refinements of polished societies."

I was tempted to point out that dancing was also popular among the less polished societies of the world. Every savage could dance. While Sir William's hints were intended to encourage me, they had the opposite effect. Already, I felt my heels digging in. I never had been one to oblige the masses for their gratification, and I would sooner refuse to dance all night in favor of observing from a quiet corner where I would assume my haughtiest look in the hope of discouraging unwanted company.

However, I would dance with Elizabeth rather than indulge my prideful inclination. It was apparent that she loved to dance, and I would please her... even if she would credit Sir William with my motive.

She looked down, fascinated with something on the floor, her cheeks a becoming shade of red. My fingers twitched to lift her chin. Instead, I extended my arm to her. "Might I have the honor of the next set?"

I did not expect her to latch onto my arm, but neither had I expected her to stare at it. She hesitated, and time seemed to stand still during the pause.

I shifted my weight awkwardly. What if she refused? I had not considered that possibility.

And yet, I should have. If our interactions had taught me anything over the past few days, it was that her behavior was impossible for me to predict.

Mrs. Bennet leaned forward, quiet for once, not even breathing, her eyes darting between me and her daughter.

With a quirk of her brow, Elizabeth said, "It depends, Mr. Darcy. Do you dance as well as you swim?"

My breath whooshed out in a breathy laugh. "Certainly better than I dive from a rope swing!"

She took my arm, and I was too happy to wince when I heard clapping behind us. Or when Mrs. Bennet said, "There will be at least one wedding at Longbourn before the end of the year!"

Elizabeth turned to face me, her brows furrowed in dismay. Even so, her eyes twinkled with the humor she wielded like a shield. I suspected that the forthcoming wedding would be mine.

By the end of the evening, I knew it.

Chapter Sixteen

15 October 1811

Dearest Georgie,

I know you expect me at Pemberley in a fortnight, but it is my greatest hope you will agree to join me at Netherfield Park at your earliest convenience instead. There is someone here I dearly wish you to meet.

With great affection,

D

18 October 1811

My Dear Brother,

Of course I shall come if you wish me to! Shall I

depart immediately, or may I wait until I complete my tutelage with the painting master you arranged to instruct me?

I am eager to meet this someone of which you speak. Dare I ask... Is this someone a she or a he?

Your curious sister,

G

18 October 1811

Dear Richard,

I just got the briefest, most intriguing message from Fitzwilliam!

He must have forgotten about the Italian painter he went to great lengths to bring to Pemberley to teach me, or he would not suggest that I travel post haste to Hertfordshire. Signore will relish the opportunity to visit his grandchildren sooner than he thought, though I have not yet mastered capturing the vivacity in a subject's eyes as he does.

I wonder if this someone I am supposed to meet has lively eyes. Please tell me, Cousin, is it a young lady? How I hope so!

Impatiently anticipating your prompt reply,

G

18 October 1811

Dearest G,

I received word from Darcy asking for me to escort you and Mrs. Annesley to Netherfield Park. His Grace extended his stay at his country residence, and I can think of no better way to spend my leave than with my favorite cousin. This message comes express in the hope that you will have sufficient time to pack before I arrive at Pemberley on the morrow.

You will like Miss Elizabeth very much, I think. She will laugh Darcy out of his sulks and tease him when he is inclined to take himself too seriously. I have never seen him smile so much as when he is in her company.

To this high praise, I must add that she is the keeper of the bravest duck in the land. The bird caused Miss Bingley a great deal of grief (for which she deserves a knighthood for her service to her fellow man... the duck, not Miss Bingley). You will love Jemima as much as you will Miss Elizabeth, I am certain.

I regret I shall have to continue to London once you are safely deposited at Netherfield Park. Your brother arranged for me to show a gentleman and his eldest son and daughter around London, insisting that I make introductions where I might. It appears the two gentlemen are both rather impressed with St. James. What do you suppose they will think of Matlock House?

I cannot help but think that this is Darcy's way of punishing me for my incessant teasing. Given my suspicion, I am determined to spare no humor or expense with the Lucases. Darcy will get no easy victory from me!

Until the morrow, poppet,

R

～

1 November 1811

Dear Cousin,

I heard from Aunt Helen today. She told me about Miss Lucas and how you made a cake of yourself over her. (Aunt's words, not mine)

Is this true? I wonder why you have made no mention of Miss Lucas in your letters. I find the omission highly suspect, Cousin. Could it be that Fitzwilliam's revenge was more effective than you are willing to admit?

Elizabeth tells me that she and Miss Lucas are very close, and that is recommendation enough for me.

You were right about Elizabeth. She is delightful, and we are already the best of friends. She has the brightest eyes! Signore should paint her. I intend to paint her likeness as a wedding present to Fitzwilliam.

I can hear you chiding me for my impatience once again, but you know as well as I do that a wedding is inevitable. Perhaps there will be a double wedding.

I speak, of course, of Mr. Bingley and Jane, not of you and Miss Lucas. I would never attempt to influence you to favor one lady over another, no matter that I think she is your perfect match and that your mother agrees. That is your choice to make, free from our influence or preference.

Speaking of agreeable ladies, if it does not rain, I am going to the stream to feed Jemima this afternoon. I do not know what transpired between her and Miss Bingley, but Jemima dotes on Fitzwilliam. She waddles behind him like a loyal dog!

Thank you for bringing me here. I have never laughed as hard as I have since coming to Netherfield Park.

When do you have more leave so that you may join us? There are many here who would be overjoyed to see you. (I refer to myself, of course. Certainly not to another lady with the name of our princess who Jemima also likes.)

Your affectionate cousin,

G

2 November 1811

Darcy,

You win. I cannot stay away a day longer. I am returning to Hertfordshire to impose on Bingley's hospitality and court Miss Lucas... if she will have an old soldier.

R

Epilogue

Ten years later

I crouched down on the limb where my father had tied a rope swing some thirty years earlier.

Elizabeth watched from the bank, dressed in head-to-toe blue flannel, holding our youngest son's hand. "Your papa has a special talent for breaking ropes."

I feigned a disgruntled growl. "The rope was old."

"That sounds familiar." Smile widening, she added, "But he is equally adept at securing new lines to tree branches."

Oliver squealed and jumped. "Papa! Papa!" He had mastered "mama" months ago, and now it was my turn to be his favorite new word. I wiggled my fingers at him and made faces.

Our oldest son pranced impatiently at the bottom of the tree. "Is it ready? I need time to practice before they get here!" Will took his role as the eldest of the cousins too seriously sometimes.

"You'll never be as good as Mama," stated our second-born as she flipped her braid over her shoulder. Janey could flip better than any of them and had nothing to prove to her cousins. She worked on a chain of daisies, and I knew I would be welcoming Rich and Bingley and their families to Pemberley with a string of flowers atop my head.

"Janey, dear, I hope you are making enough crowns for all our guests. You would not want Uncle Rich or Uncle Charlie to be jealous, would you?"

She rolled her eyes at me and pointed to a mound of flowers at the corner of her blanket. That was when I saw the daisies looped around my boots. Very pretty. "I have enough for *everyone*, Papa!"

At least I would not be the only one. *Delightful girl!* So much like her mother.

Will ran over to Elizabeth. "Mama, please, show me one more time. I am uncertain of my technique."

Janey held her hand out to Ollie, and he toddled over to her.

Elizabeth mussed Will's hair. "It does not matter so long as you are having fun, darling. You do not have to do everything perfectly."

"Please, Mama. Just once more?" he pressed.

I dropped the secured line, then dangled from the branch to make my dismount. Elizabeth was without a doubt the best rope swing acrobat in our family, but I excelled at getting everyone wet.

"Papa! Papa!" Ollie pointed and giggled.

There was only one thing to do. I had to make a splash. Letting go of the limb, I hit the water spread out as widely as my arms reached. It stung, but all three of my children laughed, and I rather liked the way my dear wife looked at me.

I rubbed my back and exaggerated my wince as I walked out of the water and onto the shore, adding a limp for good measure.

Janey draped daisies over me, Will offered to fetch the surgeon, but Ollie's suggestion was my favorite. "Mama kiss!"

"What a marvelous idea, young man!" Making sure that Ollie was secure in Elizabeth's embrace, I wrapped my arms around them to the sound of more giggles. Janey soon joined us, and I reached over to tug Will closer despite his contention that, at nine years of age, he was much too old for such parental displays of affection.

Elizabeth pecked a kiss on my temple. "Is that better, my love?"

I considered for a moment. "My forehead hurts."

She kissed my forehead.

"And my left cheek."

She kissed my cheek.

"My lip, too." I could have done this all day, but the children had had enough. Will pulled Elizabeth away and Janey returned to her mounds of flowers on the blanket with Ollie. "I have several more aches and pains, Mrs. Darcy," I called after her.

She laughed, and I anticipated the deluge of kisses she would grant me later.

Climbing as far as she could up the trunk, Elizabeth turned to me with a glorious smile that still lit my heart. And when she soared over the pond, flying and flipping to the claps and cheers of our children and recently arrived guests, I recalled the hot day at the stream where we first met.

Just as she had that day, she swam underwater until she was near to the shore. Only this time, when she emerged from the water, she walked straight to me. "You look happy, Mr. Darcy."

"*Ípe o gáidaros ton petíno kefála,* Mrs. Darcy." We laughed together, as we often did. Had there not been so many impressionable youths playing nearby, I would have stolen another kiss. Instead, I rubbed my thumb over her bottom lip. "You are dangerous."

"I should hope so, Fitzwilliam."

To make an already perfect moment truly exceptional, my delightful water nymph rose to her toes and planted a hearty kiss on my ready lips.

When love needs a helping hand—or paw—these lovable critters come to Darcy and Elizabeth's rescue.

Read all the standalone books in the Love's Little Helpers series!

Thank you!

Thank you for reading *Dangerous When Wet*! I hope you enjoyed it, and I'd love to hear your thoughts in a review on Amazon and Goodreads!

A special thanks for the wonderful people who are so important in making these stories be the best they can be. My mom (J Dawn King), who is the best first-reader and cheerleader out there! Debbie Brown, who takes my scribbles and makes them so much better! Marie Hudson, Diane Chen, and my team of ARC readers... I couldn't do what I do without your constant encouragement and support.

Want to know when my next book is available? Join my newsletter for regular updates, sales, bonus scenes, and your free novelette!

About the Author

When Jennifer isn't busy dreaming up new adventures for her favorite characters, she is learning Sign language, reading, baking (Cake is her one weakness!), or chasing her twins around the park (because ... cake).

She believes in happy endings, sweet romance, and plenty of mystery. She also believes there's enough angst on the news, so she keeps her stories light-hearted and full of hope.

She recently moved away from her home in the beautiful Andes Mountains of Ecuador with her husband and two kids to their other favorite place in the whole world, Oregon.

Connect with Jennifer!
jenniferjoywrites.com

Printed in Great Britain
by Amazon

51207995R00088